LUNA GLOBAL MEDIA

Suncrest Dv. Melbourne, FL

+1 312 212 3899 U.S.

https://lunaglobalmedia.com/

JOURNEY WITH A HEART: MIKEYS' TALE

ISBN (Paperback): 979-8-9888550-3-3

Printed in the United States of America

PREFACE

The main character is someone you know or have met. Maybe part of you had the same pain and unfulfilled dreams due to life's circumstances. As you read his story, you wonder if he will fall or find the magic he is pursuing. You will cheer for Mikey as he twists and turns through life. Generally, we have perceptions of what we want in life. Read as he will take you on his journey, and you will not want to stop reading. He will surprise you, and your heart will break at certain times of his life.

At certain stages of his life, he is a free bird. Yet, he desires to travel through life with someone as free and with a person committed to a relationship. He will be asked to fight a war that was controversial for its time and left deep scars. You will travel with the music of his time, making you remember happy times and memories.

As you read his story, you will walk with the character. You will step to the cliff's edge but then step back, inspired by his strength to carry you forward. He has been on the canvas but picked himself off the floor. His story is about a lifetime of hope, happiness, despair, and sadness. You will find yourself sitting in the same car with Mikey on the roller coaster of life. You will feel exhilarating and lose your breath at the same time.

Read and discover how and if he finds a place in life. You may reflect and see if you have arrived in your comfort zone.

DEDICATION

This story is dedicated to those who are restless and searching for something and to all the saints who died early in life due to war, illness, or tragedy. For the living, it may inspire an attitude never to give up, no matter how many curveballs come their way. The idea behind this writing is that the living give daily thanks for their blessings and that they may also do good for others.

TABLE OF CONTENTS

JOURNEY WITH A HEART
MIKEYS' TALE
BY FRANKIE

THE BEGINNING

I grew up in the Bronx, New York, in the 1950s and '60s. That period was the age of prosperity after WWII. The big band era made way for rock and roll to be heard on AM radio stations. As a result, rock-and-roll shows appeared throughout the city. New artists, like Chubby Checker, Bill Haley, and the Comets, saturated the airwaves. My favorite was Dion and the Belmonts. Dion was an Italian from DA BRONX. His group from the neighborhood around Belmont Avenue made them my favorites.

New York had three baseball teams, the Yankees, the Giants, and the Dodgers, during the 1950s. Those teams stirred up many arguments. Sometimes, we fought over who had the best team and players. I was ten when my Yankees lost to those bums from Brooklyn in 1955. If you lived in the Bronx, you were a Yankee fan or labeled a traitor if you didn't root for Mickey, Yogi, and Whitey. The following year, we avenged the loss, beat the Dodgers, and were World Series champs again. Don Larsen pitched a perfect game. Not one Dodger made it to first base, so take that, Dodger fans.

I was born to first-generation Italian-Americans, Celestina and Giuseppe Di Natale. My name is Francis Michael, but I dropped Francis when I went to first grade. The teasing and being associated with a girl's name always led to a standoff. Some kids thought I would be a pushover, and we ended up rolling on the ground. So, I learned how to use my hands and wits to not lose a fight. There were many draws, and no matter the result, you gained respect if you stood up for yourself. I started telling kids on the block that my name was Mikey, and that name has stuck throughout all these years.

I had two sisters and a younger brother. I always played in the streets, was gifted physically, and did well in sports and with my fists if needed. Arthur Avenue was the main street. Vendors sold their goods on the roads with horse-drawn wagons and pushcarts. The avenue was lined with stores. Every block had a bar. A few chairs were on the sidewalk outside each bar. Guys who wore suits and flashy rings on their fingers filled the seats. These guys are men whose profession is linked to the mafia. A wise guy is considered to be a good guy, a good fellow. He is with us (Mafia). At a tender age, I learned these guys had their own code and enforcement tactics in the neighborhood. For example, they would watch us play ball and even place a bet on which kid would win.

I was attracted to this energy because I was good physically. I gained confidence when these sharkskins suit-wearing wise guys backed me up. As I grew into my teen years, I learned that these guys controlled much of what happened in the neighborhood. The police did not bother some people who double-park a car all day. Other vehicles would get a ticket.

Big John from the corner bar asked me to bring some papers down the block to Sonny, and I was paid two dollars. My teenage friends started to imitate the wise guy's way of talking and acting. I knew I was on the wrong path. I took what I wanted, fought anyone in my way, and did illegal favors for the wise guys. I sold clothing that fell off the back of a truck. I also ran numbers for the bookies.

I knew that this was not what my parents had taught me. My parents ensured that I went to church on Sunday and had religious instruction after mass. I didn't attend Catholic grammar school because it cost too much, and I had sisters and a brother. My parents involved me in Little League, and I joined PAL (Police Athletic League). I was an excellent baseball player but liked boxing at the PAL. My parents wanted me to spend more time in this environment. They didn't want me to hang out on the corner and run errands for the guys in the shark-skinned suits.

SWEET SIXTEEN

Growing into my mid-teens, I had many boxing matches at the PAL. I was good, if I may blow my own horn. The wise guys at the boxing matches had their favorites. They offered me a professional trainer and wanted to manage me, but I declined the offer. I didn't want them to have power over me and control me.

I knew I could handle myself inside and outside the ring, but I was broadening my horizons. Music and girls began to override my pugnacious side. Before a fight and walking toward the ring, I would scan the crowd for a pretty face. I made some eye contact, and it got me some dates. I got invited to basement parties and attended the church's weekend dances to be around girls.

At sixteen, I was being swayed away from boxing and sports. Pretty girls, music, and dances were pacifying me. Doo-wop was the rave, and my friends and I would try to sing. It was very cool, although I knew I couldn't sing. The other guys singing hid my voice, and the echo in the stairway or bathroom improved the singing of the group.

Before I was sixteen, my parents wanted me to take piano lessons. That was another ploy to keep me off the street corners and tone down my ready-to-rumble attitude. But I thought "piano lessons" sounded very girly. I was probably twelve or thirteen when I refused. Nevertheless, at 16 and 17, I saw how music, singing, and playing instruments could open new doors. It especially helped me connect with girls.

My friend who learned how to play the piano was an excellent musician, and he tried to get me to play the saxophone. I had a lot of hot air, so I thought I would be successful in learning how to play. I would practice with him and other guys in his basement. I was not doing poorly and was about to graduate high school.

I lost interest and should have kept learning the saxophone. But my world expanded upon graduation. I had many dates and make-out sessions with girls. But I never had a steady girlfriend until I graduated high school. Then, I got a job in lower Manhattan, in the Wall Street area.

I worked for a brokerage house on Wall Street, and it was very mundane office-type work that didn't fit my style. But the best thing about working on Wall Street was meeting people of all ages. I met people from other parts of the city. I also met what I called the high and mighty people who lived on Long Island, Connecticut, and New Jersey. I often wondered if they lived in a refined and wealthy world. It was a step or two above my peasant existence on the streets of the Bronx.

Rubbing elbows with the privileged could be intimidating. I always believed that I could learn and survive in their world. But they could never make it on the streets of Da Bronx. I learned about life and people as I worked in the financial center of New York City. I was growing! There were plenty of good-looking women in my office. But it always seemed that I was not of interest to the girls I was interested in. Little did I realize that Rosalie had her eye on me. In my office, a group of first-year novices worked at this prestigious firm. We would go to lunch and spend our breaks together. Most of the group was like me and came from one of the five boroughs. So, my wandering eye looked outside this group because I wanted to see how the other half lived. I might have been intimidated and had to stuff paper napkins under my armpits. I didn't want my nervous perspiration to soil my shirt. I wanted to go out with a girl who would invite me to her home on Long Island. I imagined her house would have a big backyard with a swimming pool and a giant lawn. I never went to Jones Beach or the Hamptons on Long Island. But I heard all the stories about the wealth and lifestyle of its fortunate sons and daughters. I went to Orchid Beach in the Bronx, and City Island was the upscale place to hang out in the Bronx. These were my perceptions of advancing from the people and the place where I grew up.

One day, as I was going to lunch, I found myself on the elevator with a pretty girl. Rosalie and I were the only riders in the elevator. We had been in each other's company many times and were comfortable with each other. We walked to the hot dog truck and got a couple of dogs. She bought a knish and shared it with me. I discovered that she lived in Brooklyn, a world away from the Bronx. We talked about clubs we liked in our borough and places in the Village and Queens.

Rosalie had been working at the firm for a year, and I realized that she graduated high school a year before I did. We went to lunch again the next day. She asked if I had ever been to a hole-in-the-wall lunch spot a block away from our building. I said I didn't know the place but was willing to explore something new. When we arrived, a group of kids had taken their lunch break. Rosalie knew most of them because they came from Brooklyn and her neighborhood.

Rosalie was very popular and outgoing. I never saw that in her when hanging out with the group from my office. Rosalie worked in a different section from me and did messenger work. I did not like the indoor office environment. She suggested I ask my supervisor to do messenger work when needed. Most of the young kids in my office hated to do messenger work. I guess they felt it was below them. One day, her boss had many three satchels of oversized envelopes to be delivered uptown. She told her boss she needed help carrying so many large envelopes. She said she would get someone from the department next door to help. She called me, and we took the documents into the subway and made our way uptown.

It was a long trip, and after, we delivered the envelopes to an office uptown. As we were leaving the last office, I held the door open for her as she exited. Her hand touched mine as I opened the door, and I didn't perceive it as an accident. We sat closer to each other on the subway as we headed back downtown to our offices. As we got off the elevator, she thanked me for helping. To my surprise, she leaned in, kissed me on the cheek, and said, "See you tomorrow." I realized that I had been oblivious to her feelings. I began to see Rosalie as a free spirit who was sharp and bright.

The next day we ate lunch with a few people and sat together on a park bench. Rosalie was energetic and alive, and I wanted to hang out with her on the weekend to places she frequented. I would meet new people and visit new places.

After work on Friday, I went to her house in Brooklyn instead of going home to the Bronx. It was very uncomfortable to spend time at her house with her parents. Rosalie asked her parents if I could sleep on the couch downstairs. That way, I wouldn't have to travel back to the Bronx on the subway late at night. I did the same routine for a couple of weekends. Rosalie liked going to Greenwich Village and was drawn to the folk scene. That scene was new to me, and I saw a whole new world open up in front of my eyes. Rosalie had different tastes in music and even in clothing style. She was more of a jeans and sandals girl, while I had been more of the rock and roller with an eye for fashion.

We began to date every weekend, and Saturday became the implied date night. I didn't want to take the train on Friday to Brooklyn and sleep on her parents' couch. So, I decided to go out with my Bronx buddies on Friday and drive to Brooklyn on Saturday to see RoRo. That's the name that all her friends called her. I guess she was like me, not using Francis. I was Mikey, and I bought a used 1959 Chevy Impala that had been in an accident. My friend's dad owned a body and auto repair shop, and he helped repair the Chevy that took me to Brooklyn to be with RoRo. We would pick up other kids and drive out to the Bay Lounge in Rockaway or park at the beach at Riis Park. Ro was my first steady girlfriend and my first intimate relationship. We took our time before our first encounter. It happened in the back seat of the Impala on a lovers' lane in Prospect Park. I wouldn't say it was good, but we became closer after that night.

Ro and I went together for about six or seven months. Then, I decided to go to Bronx Community College for the spring semester that began in mid-January. Ro enrolled at Mercy College and started her nursing studies. It was the winter of 1964, and our last time together was around Valentine's Day. We had agreed at some point in early January that we would remain friends, but we could explore other people. We knew that going to college would open the door to new people.

Our friends always said we were like the odd couple. But we had a lot in common when we decided to change our course and go to college. We both agreed to let each other explore the new experiences that would come our way at college. We did not want to go behind each other's backs if we wanted to date a new acquaintance. That was very mature for kids who were not yet twenty years old. We respected each other and saw a different side of life during our brief relationship. RoRo and I remained friends for many years.

After my army service, we reconnected. But I'm jumping ahead of myself.

We never had a jealous streak and were honest and trusted each other. But, for some reason, we leaned on each other. It was a new experience for both of us to have our first relationship. The one thing we had in common was the spirit of adventure and freedom. We knew we didn't want to be tied down, so we mutually decided to allow ourselves to explore. We always said we would return together if we were meant to be.

EASTERN AIRLINES

I began my college career at Bronx Community College. I took nine credits as a part-time student while I continued to work on Wall Street. My friend from the neighborhood was also going to Bronx Community College (BCC), and he told me he had a tennis class with more girls than guys. He said it was a great way to pick up girls. So, I added two more credits. However I was still a part-time student because I had less than 12 credits.

Ro and I were free, so I enrolled in tennis for beginners. Being athletic, I felt I wouldn't make a fool of myself trying to hit the ball. Unfortunately, I also had that preconceived notion, and I thought tennis was a wealthy person's game played at fancy country clubs. I didn't have any tennis courts on Belmont Avenue. Handball was played against a concrete wall with cracks in it. We played with a pink Spalding rubber ball (pronounced Spaldeen). The good players played with a little black ball. I needed a glove to play with the hard black ball, so I preferred the rubber ball. The college provided the tennis racket, and I thought hitting the ball would be easier because the racket's surface was larger than my hand's palm. I was wrong about tennis. But I had made the right choice. There were about a dozen girls and only five other guys in the class.

It was a slow process, but one evening, I went to the cafeteria and saw a girl from the tennis class. I decided here was my chance and asked if anyone was sitting beside her. I knew the seat was unoccupied, but it was my opening lame line. She was pretty and had shoulder-length blond hair and blue eyes. She had a slender, firm-looking body and nice legs under her tennis uniform. I had noticed her body in class. My imagination perceived that she must be from an upscale neighborhood near East Parkchester or the Country Club section at the far eastern end of the Bronx. But she lived on LaSalle Ave., in a community of one and two-family houses. It wasn't far from the apartments on Belmont Ave., where I lived.

It had only been a few weeks since Ro and I agreed to split, and I wanted to know more about this pretty girl. At first, we talked about where we went to high school and where we lived. Then, I discovered she was like me, a child of first-generation Italians. Christina had those same core values of working to better herself, and that family is at the center of everything. She had a younger brother and older sister, and she went to work at the Bronx Zoo upon graduating high school. Chris went to a Catholic high school and was a star as a track team member. She was taking some night courses to get ahead and get a better job at the corporate level at the Zoo.

We started going out on the weekends but didn't rush into anything. Christina had many girlfriends in high school. She went out with them on a Friday night. We didn't smother ourselves by seeing each other for an entire weekend. Instead, we would often go out with some of her friends or hang out with some of my buddies from the neighborhood.

Chris and I were turning 19 in April 1964. Our real-life experiences and family upbringing influenced our thinking about the future at this stage of life. Boy, I had a lot of perceptions of what life should look like. I needed to work to make money to buy things and travel. I wanted more out of life than to be a nine-to-five guy who had to support a family. But I also wanted a companion or two who shared my thoughts.

People have always asked since I was a senior in high school, what do you want to be? That question annoyed me, and I had no clue how to answer those inquiring minds. I wouldn't be a boxer, and although it looked glamorous, I didn't want a life as a wise guy. I wanted to travel, see new places, and meet people. I would find that special girl who wanted the same things out of life. I didn't want to get married. I had people to meet and places to go.

One evening at school, Chris told me she saw a notice on the bulletin board about jobs with Eastern Airlines. Eastern had a program that reached out to college students for a career in the airline industry. Some programs would even pay for part or all of your college tuition. The airlines also had good benefits; one significant benefit was discounts on airfares. All this appealed to me, especially the ability to travel. So, I called the number on the notice and made an appointment for an interview.

I saw no future in my Wall Street job, and LaGuardia Airport wasn't far from my home. I thought, no more rush hour crowds on the subway, doing mundane tasks, or being a messenger. I didn't know what job I wanted with the airlines, but I knew I didn't want to be a baggage handler or to sit behind a desk. I thought I was good with my hands, had worked on autos, and didn't mind getting dirty. I discovered a few job openings with the ground crew during the interview. It was an outdoor job on the tarmac, and the work involved refueling planes and learning some of the mechanics. At some point, I would be able to guide a plane into a gate or onto the runways. That sounded good, and I would begin work in a couple of weeks. The pay was about the same as my Wall Street gig, but Eastern would pay for some tuition on specific courses. There would be a probationary period. But if I completed it, I would get airfare discounts under certain conditions. I began my new apprentice job in the middle of April and I just turned 19. Chris and I got along well, and although we weren't a couple, but I wanted to focus on her. Working at Eastern Airlines was a happy time in my life. It was a new job that I thought would last a long time. I also hoped Chris and I would develop a relationship that would last.

THE RELATIONSHIP

School ended in late May, and I increased my frequency of being with Chris. Finally, at the end of June, I passed my probation at Eastern. I began working and learning the ropes of minor plane maintenance. Most planes were propeller-driven then, and I was excited to learn the mechanics. I thought I had found the answer to what I wanted to be when I was growing up. It was no great calling that I wanted to be an airline mechanic, but it seemed to work out that way. I was happy with the job, and more importantly, Chris and I seemed to be advancing our careers. Chris entered the sales and marketing department at the Zoo. We focused on our jobs, and we applied ourselves at work. The result was making more money so we could have fun.

I spent more time with her family, and she did likewise with mine. Our parents approved, and I began to feel the pressure from aunts and uncles and my parents. They had asked that dumb question, "What do you want to be?" Now, they were hinting that this was the girl I would settle down with. They wanted me to be like my parents and have a family. OH NO!

Chris was getting the same vibrations. Her mom and grandmother liked me. I could feel that, but dad was protective of his baby girl, and I also felt that. I still had to pick her up at her house and not meet her on the corner, as I had done with other girls. We did steam up the windows of my Impala, but we would always get to that point where she would remove my wandering hand. I was OK with that because I felt connected with her, and we always had a good time together no matter what we did. During that summer, we went to the movies, which always gave us a warm and cozy feeling. Sometimes, we went to a Yankee game or caught a singing group. One of the best shows we saw was a girl group program featuring the Shirelles and Martha & the Vandellas. We were experiencing many new things for the first time together. There were many "firsts," but we never went all the way.

We complimented each other. We started to talk about going to the Catskills for an overnight trip. We knew this would not go over well, especially with her dad. So, we talked about making a day trip up to Exit 20 on the NY Thruway to the Catskill game farm and other attractions. I would buy her a stuffed animal, and she would buy lunch. We were a great team. I never wanted that

17

to end, although I didn't know if she would grow tired of me.

We discussed that marriage was way down the road, if at all, in our immediate future. But, heck, we hadn't even gone all the way, so thinking about marriage and kids was far removed from our minds. We both kept the door open for many options, but something between us kept us exclusive to each other.

The summer had gone, and the fall and the holidays would be upon us. I started to think about what I should get her for Christmas. I anticipated us being closer and experiencing our first Christmas together. Christina's job was organizing a company ski trip to Hunter Mountain. It was set for the first weekend in December. We took many day trips up the Thruway to exit twenty, and Chris was familiar with the Catskill game farm and had made several trips to the Catskill region. It was a few minutes from Hunter Mountain, and there would be snow in December. I was sure it would be picturesque, like a scene on a Hallmark greeting card. That kid from the steamy streets in the Bronx was going green and smelling the cool, clean air of the mountains.

Christina's friend at work made the room assignments. The specific room assignments had an ulterior motive. They were designed to ensure that couples had the potential for a sleepover. A log cabin had two rooms with an adjoining door that separated them. Each room had two beds, so the accommodation was set for two girls in one room and two guys in another.

Annie, Chris's friend at work, would be her roommate. Annie's boyfriend and I would bunk in the adjoining room. At least, that was the perception created when employees saw the room assignments. But parents knew nothing of adjoining rooms or the real roommates for the weekend.

At the time, I wasn't sure we would have sex. But I went to the drugstore to buy a box of Trojans condoms, the brand of choice for protection. By now, I had done this several times before. So, I was no longer embarrassed to ask the druggist for the box of protection with other people standing around. That was one of those life lessons guys had to go through.

I remember the first couple of times I purchased a pack of condoms. If people were at the counter, I would act as if I were shopping in an aisle. All the while, I had my eye on the counter, and when no one was around, I hurried up to the counter and asked for a pack of Trojans. First, the druggist would ask, "Do you want a three-pack, six-pack, or a dozen?" Then, he would ask if I wanted them pre-lubed, and I would feel the heat rush up my neck to my face. I was sure my face turned candy apple red. I hoped the transaction was over before a customer approached.

I knew that the druggist was playing with my head. A dozen! I learned these things from listening to guys on the corner. I also heard the wise guys talk about their exploits. And being with some girls with more experience than a 17-year-old is how I learned the ropes. But those first few encounters at the drugstore were very stressful. I was past that embarrassment, and my anxiety was now over Chris and me sleeping together for the first time.

That weekend ski trip was as perfect as I could expect, and we rode back on the bus with Chris snuggled up to my shoulder. Perfect, until I got home.

GREETINGS

I returned home from the ski trip on Sunday night. A letter from my Uncle Sam greeted me. It arrived on Saturday. It was a notice to appear for a physical screening to determine if I was fit for military service. President Kennedy had been assassinated in November 1963, but he had sent support troops to aid the South Vietnamese Army in their struggle to fight the North Vietnamese. I didn't know he had built up support troops in Southeast Asia. The troops were meant to help the government of South Vietnam. He aimed to help defeat a communist takeover. I enrolled at Bronx Community College, began a new job, and had a special relationship with Chris, but my life would be altered when I got the notice to appear for a physical. Two of my friends had received the same message to appear, but only one guy, Joey, got drafted into the Marines. He was in boot camp, and my other friend wasn't called. I didn't get too concerned. I didn't know that the US was preparing to escalate our involvement in Vietnam.

Chris and I had just taken our relationship to a higher level and slept together for the first time. I went for my physical in the middle of December, and because it was the holidays, I forgot about the draft. Chris and I would be with each other and our families. At the time, that's all that mattered.

I had not bought her anything for Christmas, but after the ski trip weekend, I felt my gift would need to be unique. So, I went to a jeweler on Arthur Ave. He had two businesses—one with the general public and one with the wise guys. I asked one of my friends, Johnny, who hung around the avenue and did favors for the wise guys if he knew a good jeweler who wouldn't rip me off. I had no idea what to look for and didn't have much money. I wanted something special for Chris that wouldn't break the bank. Worst yet, I didn't want to get beat and find out I gave her a piece of worthless jewelry.

Johnny took me to Sal the Jeweler and told him he was a friend of his, which was code for he's a good guy, one of us; take care of him. A ring was not a good choice because I didn't know her size and didn't want to have to guess at that. Chris had a gold chain with a cross around her neck. I remember her telling me that her grandmother gave it to her as a graduation gift. My price range was low. Sal asked if a charm would be a good gift. She could add it to her chain with the cross.

Sal took out a tray from the glass counter with many different charms. I liked a heart and asked how much. He said I could have it for ten bucks. Although ten bucks was a lot of money at the time, I wanted something more unique. Sal asked what her birthstone was, and I knew it was an emerald. I learned that from Ro because she was into astrology, the stars, and birthday signs.

Sal suggested he could put a tiny emerald on the heart. He told me the 14k gold heart with the emerald setting would cost about twenty dollars. He showed me what it would look like, and I thought it was sending the perfect message to her. The heart was half the size of her cross, and the emerald set at the top of the heart was noticeable. I told him I didn't have twenty dollars to pay him. He told me to give him $10 now and pay him the other $10 before Christmas. He told me to return in three days, and he would have the heart and emerald ready.

It was a great gift, although $20 was almost half my take-home salary. I didn't think Sal was giving anything away. But I knew he wasn't beating me. I got the wise guy's price. Besides, he gave me a couple of weeks to pay.

The following two weeks turned into a whirlwind. First, I had to pay Sal, and then on Christmas Eve, I got a letter from the War Department to report for basic training after the New Year. The usual course of events around Christmas was always hectic, and now I had to think about leaving Chris to join the army.

On top of that, my relationship and romance with Christina and her family were growing. So, even though I was shocked to receive my draft notice on Christmas Eve, it didn't hit home. I blocked it out of my mind. I anticipated everything that would happen in the next several hours.

Tradition would dictate that around 5 p.m., my family would gather in my grandmother's 6-room apartment. All this food coming out of my grandma's little kitchen amazed me and made me feel dizzy. The extravaganza lasted for hours. Around coffee time, some presents were exchanged.

There were no significant gifts, and giving and sharing were paramount. I was getting fidgety. I was committed to stopping at Christina's house. I wanted to wish her family a Merry Christmas Eve. I was invited there the next day for Christmas Day dinner. Christina and I had planned to attend midnight mass with several friends. We had to fulfill our family's obligatory appearances. But we couldn't wait to hold hands and see our friends at night.

I kept thinking about when I should give Chris my present. I thought giving a Christmas gift on Christmas Day was more appropriate. That meant she would open my present in front of her family. The heart with the emerald chip was so personal to me, and I wanted to give her the gift when we were alone. We stood at the back of the church; it was a standing room only. I whispered in her ear that I wanted to give her my present after church. I asked if that was ok. Chris told me it would be fine to get her present after church, but I would have to wait for my gift from her the next day at dinner. I said I didn't mind waiting. I told her it would be Christmas day by the time I gave her my present after the mass.

As mass was ending, Chris and I and a couple of friends left to beat the crowd out the door. We decided to go to the back of the schoolyard next to the church and hang out. Her friend Roxy and her boyfriend brought a bottle of wine. We passed the bottle around and shared a Christmas drink. After we all had a couple of swings at the bottle of Bolla Valpolicella, I gave Chris her present. We were in the shadows to avoid being seen. I told her to move to the yard's side so the street light could help her see my gift.

She was excited, and she knew it had to be jewelry because of the lovely packaging. I gave her the tiny box that my sister wrapped, and Chris looked at her friend wide-eyed. We moved to the fence, where she could get a better look at the contents of this little box. I was more excited than Chris, and I wanted to see her reaction. When she saw it, she said it was beautiful, and with her free hand, she pulled me toward her and kissed me. She immediately showed Roxy, and their heads nodded approval. Mission accomplished! I was so happy.

It was getting late, and I walked Chris home, got in my Impala, and headed home. As I got into bed, all the events kept my mind off the letter I had received less than 24 hours ago about the draft. I still had to get through

Christmas day, and my mind didn't have time to dwell on what would happen after the New Year.

On Christmas morning, my sisters would start the coffee, and I would run several blocks down to the bakery on Arthur Avenue to beat the crowd. I'd return home with warm buns, crullers, and donuts. By now, my sisters had the coffee going and were making scrambled eggs and bacon. As little kids, we always got up first and snooped under the tree to see what Santa Claus had left. We had to wait for our parents to get up and make breakfast. Now, my older sisters decided it was time to make breakfast for our parents. Our parents had made Christmas special for us so many times when we were growing up.

Christmas day was as hectic as Christmas Eve and the days leading up to Christmas. After breakfast and exchanging our gifts, we all had to get washed and dressed. We had to see my father's parents and exchange gifts over a drink. We would also stop at my dad's brother's house to have another drink and wish each other a happy holiday. That had to be done by 1 pm because it was back to the other grandmother's house for dinner. It was no tiny feat for a family of six to get ready with one full bath and a half bath.

I also knew I had to attend dinner at Chris's home. My dad kept us on schedule. We returned to Grandma's before 1 p.m. I was excused from the table because I was having dinner at Chris' house. I did have to shake hands with my uncles and kiss my aunts while their hands pinched my cheeks. They always did that since I was a kid, and my aunts didn't realize how hard they pinched my face.

I was happy to leave after grabbing a couple of meatballs, and I arrived at Chris's a little past two p.m., which was not a big deal. Their family had exchanged gifts in the morning, and Chris gave me her present before we sat at the table. Chris was wearing her gold cross, and she had added my heart to the chain. Her mom said it was a lovely present and looked good on the chain with the cross.

I opened her gift. It was a silver bracelet with a nameplate inscribed with MIKEY. Chris later said that she didn't know what to get me. Her mom suggested a shirt or gloves. But Chris wanted something more personal than clothing. So, she decided on something I could always wear.

As dinner was ending, all that anticipation for Christmas was behind me. The next event would be New Year's Eve. It paled in preparation for Christmas with all its family traditions. I was sitting on the couch with Chris, and my mind wandered about what would happen after New Year's. I realized that I would not have many more opportunities to sit with Chris or hold her hand. I would miss her warm touch. We had our first and only sexual encounter three weeks ago. I wondered if we would stay together.

I saw that stupid letter in my mind's eye from the war department saying greetings. How ironic! It was the season to be jolly, and it was. Greetings conveyed all the good feelings of the Christmas season. So, how would a letter like this be a happy greeting? The following weeks would give me some answers about my relationship with Chris. Greetings?

I had no idea how 1965 would greet me. I couldn't think about New Year's Eve. My mind kept thinking that by the end of the month, I would be taking the train to Whitehall Street in lower Manhattan to be sworn into the army.

YOU'RE IN THE ARMY

On January 28, I was on the Lexington Ave. Express train. It was early morning, and the rush hour was underway. My destination was the military induction center on Whitehall Street in Lower Manhattan. One year ago, it would have been a typical workday, and I would be heading to my job on Wall Street. I boarded the train's last car, as it was my habit. I went to the rear and stood with my back to the motorman's door. When I boarded the train, it usually had a few empty seats. I never took an open seat because, after a few stops, the train would have straphangers. I would give up my seat to a lady if she were standing. The leather straps hung above the standing riders. They held onto the straps when the train was moving. If you were short, I was 5'7"; it was a stretch to reach the strap. I always felt uncomfortable with all the twists of the tracks. I especially felt this way when the train was packed with people. At times, you could find yourself crunched with a stranger, and it could be awkward if you were face to face with a pretty girl. By the time the train got to midtown Manhattan, you would be packed like a sardine. For these reasons, I retreated to the back door of the train. I could lean against the door. The train was elevated for a few stops, and I could look out the rear window of the train.

On my way to the Army induction center, I walked to the train station at East 183rd St. and Jerome Ave. I hopped on the Lexington Ave express train toward Yankee Stadium. After the stop at the stadium, the train would travel underground as it made its way to Brooklyn. The subway was an excellent means of transportation. But, the cars and stations were dirty and covered in graffiti. New Yorkers thought it was normal and accepted the conditions. Today's ride would be my last for a while. It was a one-way trip to the induction center. I didn't have much information except to report at 8 a.m. and to bring a small overnight bag with some toiletries. I had shaving cream, a razor, a toothbrush, and toothpaste. My mom packed some tissues and packed an extra pair of underwear. I could always count on clean underwear. Did your mother always tell you to wear clean underwear in the event you had to go to the hospital? I never understood her logic. If I had an emergency and was rushed to the hospital, I didn't think the doctors and nurses would be focused on my briefs.

I watched from the back window of the train. The train had left the Yankee Stadium station at 161st Street and River. It was descending from its elevation, and the stadium was fading away. In seconds, the stadium was gone, and the train plunged into the darkness of the subway. I wondered when I would see another Yankee game. I don't remember much of the ride downtown, but I was anxious. I couldn't wait to get on my journey into the military. In January 1965, I was oblivious to our country's involvement in Vietnam. My dad and uncles had served in WWII. At that time, Americans were expected to be drafted or enlist in the military as a duty. But this army thing interrupted my life. I had been growing at work and in my relationship with Christina. I tried not to be angry. I would do my two years, return to work at Easter Airlines, and resume my life with Christina.

Sometime between Christmas Day and when I left home to be inducted into the military. Chris and I rented a motel room and had our second round of lovemaking. We were much more comfortable with each other, and we talked about my leaving for the army. Chris swore she would wait for me, and I told her I wouldn't be angry if she wanted to date another guy. I only asked that she be honest. She insisted that she would never cheat, nor did she ever wish to be with anyone else. I felt the warm mist run down her face; my eyes welled up, and I fought to hold back a tear. Wow, this tough kid from the Bronx is almost crying and doing it in front of another person. Like my father and his generation that went to war, they returned to the girl of their dreams. Perhaps I watched too many war movies on a Sunday afternoon. John Wayne usually won the war and returned to the girl of his dreams. My mind wandered as I stood on the Lexington Ave. Express train as it rambled toward Whitehall Street. Finally, it was my turn to get off the train. Those sweet and tender thoughts of being with Chris carried me to the induction center.

I arrived at the center and got on line. That would be the first of many lines I stood on as I waited for the next instruction. I gave my name to a clerk at the front desk. She handed me an envelope, and I was told to sit in the next room. I was told not to open the envelope. I did as told and entered a room filled with chairs; about half were filled with other young men. It was quiet until an officer appeared in a starched and pressed uniform. He yelled, "On your feet." I heard the rumble of feet moving as everyone quickly jumped to attention. The officer welcomed us to military service for our country. He told us that a bus would take us to Fort Dix in New Jersey, and we would be instructed on our next step. We raised our right hand and swore to protect and defend the United States. I don't remember the exact words. But I remembered the officer congratulating the thirty baby-faced, wide-eyed, unsuspecting recruits. I felt anticipation and sweat running down my arms. The process seemed very organized. We boarded the bus and were hustled to Fort Dix. I had never been outside of New York. The five boroughs, Long Island, and up the New York State Thruway as far as exit 21 were my worldly experiences. The bus pulled away from the curb and headed up the West Side Highway. I saw the sign for the Holland Tunnel. I had never been in the Holland Tunnel but had been through the Brooklyn Battery Tunnel. The bus ride was about an hour, maybe longer, and the bus carried us through the main gate at Fort Dix.

You could have heard a pin drop as the recruits gawked at the wooden buildings. All the buildings looked the same. The grounds were clean and free of any debris. I was use to seeing garbage on the streets in New York City. The bus stopped, and I heard the door open. The yelling and drama began when a Sgt. jumped up the stairs of the bus and told us to get our sorry asses off the bus. As I hurried to get off with the other recruits and reached the bottom step, another soldier yelled for us to "fall in." Two other soldiers were waiting for us. The term "fall in" was the first of many army terms I would learn. It didn't take a genius to figure out what it meant. The welcoming committee yelled at the recruits to hurry up. We were told to move our sorry asses. I was among the first ten recruits to get off the bus. It was a quick dash to the other sergeants, who set the recruits in a formation if needed. By the time everyone was off the bus, we were standing in three lines, one behind the other. The Sgt. in charge said, "Listen up." That was another term I would hear many times. He told recruits to listen for their names and proceed to one of two lines. He further explained that each line would embark on a military vehicle. The vehicle would take us to a location on the base. Then, we would get further orders. He said the information in our envelopes would tell us our final destination. I was told not to open the envelopes until instructed.

The Sgt. asked if we understood. Most of us shook our heads, prompting the irritated Sgt. to yell at us. He asked again, and someone yelled yes, sir. It may have been a polite response, but the Sgt. got in the kid's face. "Yes, sir," and he yelled, "Do you see any bars on this uniform?" I knew from watching war movies that officers had silver or gold bars on their lapels. Sergeants had stripes. I thought the kid was going to puke or pee in his pants. The Sgt made him say several times No Sgt or Yes Sgt. It was another lesson learned at someone's expense.

My name was called, and I boarded an army bus, as did most other recruits. Four or five other recruits boarded a smaller army vehicle. I wondered where they were going. I found out that my bus was going to McGuire Air Force Base, which was adjacent to Fort Dix. I was hustled off the bus again and lined up in formation. Listen up was the command, and I listened for my name to be called. The sergeant said to open the letter and verify the training center. He called out my name and said I would attend basic training in Fort Benning, Ga., and board a military flight. The flight would be leaving at a specific time. I don't recall the time. I would head for the waiting area on the tarmac designated as Ft. Benning. The suspense was over. I hoped to do my basics at Fort Dix and be close to home. Oh well, I always liked the adventure of traveling, and the army fulfilled those wishes.

In less than an hour, I was sitting with the other recruits on the Ft. Benning line. I boarded a cargo-type plane, and we sat across from each other. That was my first plane ride, and I thought it was pretty cool. The plane stopped in South Carolina, and a group of recruits got off and headed for Fort Jackson. I stayed on board, and the plane took to the sky for its final destination. I landed and was again told to hustle onto another military bus. I was welcomed to the Infantry Training Center. My trip started on 183rd St. and Jerome Ave. and ended in the deep south, which looked nothing like the Bronx.

THE BASICS

My first day in the army was quite long, and I experienced many different emotions. It was mid-afternoon on Thursday, January 28, but I felt like I had been awake for two days. I was standing in formation at the reception center at Ft. Benning, and it was another listen-up moment. My name was called. The second platoon in Company B was my assignment. I belonged to the 1st or 2nd infantry training brigade. I don't remember. I only had to remember to get off when the bus stopped at Company B. I got off with about thirty or forty other recruits. I met my drill sergeant. Sgt. Joe Davis had four stripes, and he could have been the poster boy of the perfectly dressed soldier. Back then, white society would have referred to Sgt. Davis, a black man, as colored. His uniform was perfectly starched. Every crease was perfect, down to his bloused pant bottoms which rode atop his black combat boots that were polished and shined. On the left side of his uniform was a blue-and-white logo. It looked like a long rifle with a wreath around it. Above that was another sewn-on insignia of wings with a parachute in its center. On the right side of his shirt was his name in yellow, Davis. I could tell this guy was the real deal soldier.

Two other sergeants were part of the cadre of the second platoon. Sgt. Pritchard was young-looking and had wings on his shirt over his left breast. The other sergeant's name was Melendez. They had the same symbols on their uniforms that Sgt Davis had, except they had three stripes. I would later discover the names of these badges. The rifle was a musket from the Revolutionary War period. It is set against a blue background, and a wreath surrounds it. The badge is awarded to infantry soldiers whose unit is engaged in combat operations. The Combat Infantryman's Badge (CIB) is a proudly worn badge of honor. The other badge was a pair of wings curved inward and showed an open parachute. It is the symbol earned for being a paratrooper (airborne soldier). Those who attend "jump school" and pass a three-week physical endurance assault earn their wings if they pass the required five jumps. Once a soldier receives his wings, he is said to be no longer a leg.

There was a lot of activity, and I made the first stop at the medical center. They gave us a quick exam and administered several vaccinations to us. After that, in the next room, I received my military haircut. Now, that was a very traumatic episode for me. I didn't look good in a buzz cut, and I always hated it when my dad took me to the barber shop for a crew cut. The crew cut was selected because my dad didn't have to take me to the barbershop as often and pay the barber. There were times when my grandfather would give the grandkids the same haircut. I was marched down the hallway and was given bedding: two sheets and a blanket. I stuck out my arms and moved on down the line. The supply Sgt looked at me and said medium and a soldier added white underwear to the pile. Next, I was given a couple of uniforms that I was sure would be baggy. I felt like joking and asking for a 32 waist and 30-inch length for the pants and a size 39 short for the shirt. But I decided to keep my mouth shut. I was given combat boots, a field jacket with liner, gloves, socks, and a baseball cap to cover my bald head. I could barely hold all these items, and the supply Sgt said I would receive more stuff tomorrow. They handed me a small bag containing a shaving kit, a toothbrush with toothpaste, a set of dog tags, and name tags. I had to sew the name tags onto my uniform. Who the heck was going to sew?

I was told to head for the barracks at the bottom of the hill for Company B. Other sergeants from Company B were down the hill. They told us to double-time (run). Luckily, I was handed a duffle bag to store my new wardrobe and bedding. I double-timed to my barracks. Once inside the barracks, Sgt. Davis directed me to my bunk. I had a lower bed in the center of the room. Ten bunk beds were on each side of the room; twenty bunk beds accommodated 40 soldiers. These recruits were soldiers in the 2nd platoon. Each soldier had a foot locker and a wall locker, and our sergeants taught us which items to hang in the wall locker. They also showed us how to arrange our foot locker. The army had a prescribed system of how you faced your toothbrush and how you stored each item.

Sgt. Davis told the recruits that they should help each other because there were sure to be a lot of mistakes. He told us he would review and inspect our lockers the next day and see how we did as individuals and as a unit. He said we didn't have much time to waste today and had to "get to gettin'." That expression was one of his favorites. If you were falling behind in a task, he would address the recruits, "Boy, you better get to gettin'." Sgt. Davis told us to gather in the center of the room and watch Sgt. Pritchard and Sgt.

Melendez make a bed. The emphasis was on uniformity. The folds of the sheets and blankets had to be tight, and I heard the term hospital corner for the first time. That term was used to describe how the bottom ends and bottom sides of the sheets were folded. It's funny, but I still remember exactly how to make hospital corners after all these years. I still make my bed using the same technique, albeit not as tight as when I was in the army.

Sgt. Davis showed us the bathrooms, but the only acceptable term for the bathroom was called the latrine. The latrine looked cold, with primarily white tiles and black tiles. On one side was a row of sinks, and on the other side, facing the sinks, was a row of toilets. The toilets did not have partitions, so there was no privacy. At the end of the latrine was one large room with several showerheads, so about a dozen guys could shower at once. The army even had a prescribed way of taking a shower. You turn on the water for about thirty seconds to get wet, then turn the water off, lather up, and turn the water on to rinse off. The whole process would take less than three minutes. Sgt. Davis also told us that the latrine would be scrubbed and polished every morning. The barracks floor would be, too.

By now, it was dark outside, and Sgt Davis, along with Sgt Pritchard and Melendez, marched us to the mess hall for our first meal. The army had a system to follow when entering the mess hall. Everyone formed a single line and faced the mess hall. The recruits were not permitted to move around or talk. I had to stand in a parade rest position. I stood with my feet shoulder-width apart, and my thumbs were interwoven and rested on the small of my back. Each time a soldier entered the mess hall, the line would move up. But to move forward, I had to come to the position of attention. Then a left face, a right face, and back to the parade rest. I did this until I was at the front door of the mess hall.

While waiting to enter, a cadre member might ask a soldier what his 1st general order was. We would learn a bunch of general orders, and God help us if we forgot any one of them. Each recruit had an identification number with a prefix before it. A recruit who enlisted was an RA (regular army-professional soldier). I was drafted, and all draftees were US, which signified being conscripted. I would be asked to recite my ID number. If I forgot, I had to go to the back of the line or drop and give the Sgt. 25 pushups. On the first day, we were all given a break. But they told us to remember our number and general orders from that day forward.

Chow is the Army term for food. It wasn't bad. You could ask for anything offered, but whatever I put on my plate, I had better finish it. There was always bread and dessert. Kool-Aid seemed to be an everyday favorite. Breakfast was the best meal of the day. The platoon learned that it was helpful to be the first or second platoon to enter the mess hall. This was especially true for breakfast. Breakfast always had bacon, sausage, and eggs. Pancakes and French toast, oatmeal, and grits were regular choices. The cooks did a fantastic job because a company usually has 160 recruits plus the cadre. The mess hall couldn't accommodate 200 soldiers at one time. So, the best-performing platoon on the previous day got to eat first. Hence, the concept of teamwork and competition was instilled in me with breakfast. I mentioned the cooks did a great job feeding so many, and the entire process took less than an hour. Being served last meant that a large amount of grease had been used for the first hundred soldiers, and you might hit a greasy patch. Greasy food didn't help a soldier, especially in the field. There was no time to waste in the morning, and everything we did was done quickly. We had to make bunks and ensure lockers were neat and in order. The barracks had to be clean, and the floors were polished or buffed daily. The latrine had to be mopped and cleaned. Around 6:30, our sergeants would inspect the barracks, our lockers, and our appearance. At 7 am, the four platoons would be in a company formation and begin a training day.

The lights were out by 10 p.m. if I remember correctly, and that first night, I slept like a baby. I was told that Friday would be another day to get more gear. We'd also revisit how to fall in formation. We'd also review how to wear the uniform. We'd also practice some basic marching and facing movements. The next day, I was fitted for my dress uniform and khakis. These uniforms were needed for travel and our graduation. I was issued a helmet with a liner and web gear with a canteen. I was also given a knapsack with an entrenching tool (a foldable shovel). We practiced our facing and marching movements. We did some PT (physical training) that would be part of our everyday routine.

Saturday would officially start basic training, and Sunday would be a rest day. The military had great respect for soldiers wishing to attend their church services. There were several churches of various denominations. We were all encouraged to take part in a service. But Sunday church days have been less frequent since I graduated high school. I had become one of those Sunday Catholics when I could make it. Still, I had a strong faith in God. But, I thought some of the manufactured rules of the religion didn't make sense. Old habits die hard, and I always carry a miraculous medal in my wallet. I wore it occasionally, but as I got older, I wore it less and placed it in my wallet. I also carried a prayer card. It was the prayer of St. Francis of Assisi. I hated my name at an early age. But, in a religious instruction class, I read about Francis of Assisi. I carried the Francis of Assisi prayer card to make amends for my shallow thinking. I never used that name.

I went to church that first Sunday. As usual, I drifted off when the priest gave his sermon. My mind floated back to all the good times I had with Chris. I realized that I hadn't thought much about her since Thursday, the day I left for the army. I started to believe that she would never last as my girlfriend.

My first Sunday at Ft. Benning ended, and the grind of training began on Monday. The training lasted about eight weeks. I wondered what was in store for me. I was ready to become a soldier and wanted to absorb all I could and do my best.

JUMP SCHOOL

Some recruits were asked during basic training if they wanted to become paratroopers. I always looked for adventure and new experiences, so I said yes. That class would start one week after basic training. I would do my advanced individual training after completing jump school. The orientation for jump school began on Saturday. I received new gear and some material to read about what to expect and the history of the paratrooper. I had to follow the same procedures concerning my lockers and keeping the barracks clean.

The class was told that half of us could be dropouts. I had to complete five jumps from a plane and pass all the physical requirements. That included a one and a two-mile run that had to be completed within a specific time. If a soldier failed the first run, he would get a second shot to pass the next day. Two strikes and the trainee would find himself reassigned. My class had about eighty soldiers, divided into two platoons.

Monday was my first training day. Our platoon leader wasn't exaggerating. The physical demands were much tougher compared to basic training. The platoons were marched to the PT field, and we warmed up with a half-mile run. Calisthenics followed, and the army's favorite exercise, the pushup, was on the menu. In basic training, almost everything was twenty pushups in a set. We might do two or three sets, with a rest between each set. In jump school, the expectation for my platoon was always, "Give me fifty." We were airborne and better than all the rest.

Not so fast claiming to be the best. I had to prove I was among the best. The trainees had three demanding weeks of training, and I would earn the airborne title and get my wings only if I could beat all the tests. The first afternoon of training started with classroom instruction. Then, our class went back to the PT field for a run. As the week continued, we jumped from a stationary landing about four feet off the ground. Then, we graduated to a higher level. The instructors emphasized not landing stiff-legged. When we jumped with all our gear, we could injure our knees and ankles. It was OK to fall and roll; the goal was not to land standing up; it was to land safely. The concept was to land as soft as possible and on your toes rather than driving your heels into the earth. This would prevent sprains, strains, and, even worse, fractures.

By day two, the mile and two-mile qualifying times were in the books. Nine trainees from my platoon didn't make the required time. The second platoon also lost a similar number for the same reason. There were plenty of aches and pains. If you sprained something, you kept your mouth shut. We ate the pain unless we couldn't walk or use our arms. There was no sick call, so you were out of school if you claimed you were ill.

The next test was jumping from a two-hundred-and-fifty-foot tower. The jumpers wore a harness and parachute. It didn't sound like a big deal until you got to the top and looked down. We lost a couple more trainees because they froze when it was their turn to jump. If you ever stood on the roof of a three-story building and looked over the edge, you could feel a bit uncomfortable. Looking down from a 250-foot platform was like looking down from a Wall Street building. This experience was similar to the parachute ride at Coney Island. The jump was controlled, and the biggest fear was looking down. I made several jumps from the tower; the first two were without gear. For the last jump from the tower, I had a full load. That jump produced two more casualties. A broken leg and a fractured arm eliminated two more trainees. My third and last week of jump school began on Saturday. It would be my first of five jumps from a plane. That last week, known as jump week, is what I and all the trainees worked towards.

The instructors told us we would perform all five jumps at approximately 1300 feet. We would be hitting the ground at about 13 MPH. My first exit from a plane was a no-frills jump, known as a Hollywood Jump, and I had only a parachute and a reserve chute. I carried some gear on my body as I continued to jump. The last jump was with complete equipment and weapons.

If anyone told you, they had no anxiety or fear they were dishonest. Of course, the instructors explained what would happen while I was firmly on the ground. I kept telling myself it was no big deal, but I was in a classroom. Even when I boarded the propeller-winged plane, I didn't fully grasp what I would feel. I wondered how I would feel when I jumped from a moving plane at 1300 feet. The plane was noisy, but I worked at Eastern Airlines. I had heard the loud hum of propellers.

I left the safety of the classroom with the other trainees and walked through the empty airplane hangar onto the tarmac. A large four-engine prop plane sat there, waiting to take us on our first jump.

The wide-eyed jump school candidates boarded the plane and flew up into the wild blue yonder. The green light came on. I stood to hook up to the static line with the rest of my platoon. The door opened. The rush of air, combined with the noise of the engine's propellers, was almost deafening. I dare anyone to say they didn't take a deep gulp. When a soldier stood at the doorway, he would get a tap on the shoulder and walk out into the sky. As the line moved and I got closer to the door, a soldier unhooked himself, sat down, and refused to jump. The rest of us passed him by. I kept telling myself not to think or look down. Wait for the tap, yell Geronimo, and step into the air.

I jumped, and it felt like my stomach had dropped. I lost my breath but was jolted to reality when the chute opened. The static line I hooked up to was the automatic trigger that deployed my parachute. I only had to fold my arms and step into the air. I saw the canopy above me and the blue sky around me. I floated toward the earth, and in the last hundred feet, the ground was coming up at me. I bent my knees. As soon as my feet touched the ground, I leaned to the side to avoid absorbing the shock and weight on my legs. I made it. I wanted to do it again because it was like the thrill I felt when I first rode the roller coaster at Coney Island. I would make four more jumps. At some point, the jumps were performed in full gear. My platoon and I had made three more jumps, and no one was injured or chickened out. The last jump was at hand. It would be in full battle gear with a weapon.

Finally, the soldiers who made the last jump were safely on the ground. We had all made it. I remember our instructors being so happy and proud that we had made it. I can't remember or describe the feeling of self-accomplishment and brotherhood. It all seemed to blend together. Out of the eighty or so soldiers who went to jump school, a little over 50 survived. We boarded the deuce-in-a-half vehicles waiting for us at the landing zone and got a ride back to the barracks. I guess we deserved that ride instead of marching back.

After arriving at the barracks, both platoons were told to fall in. The joy and euphoria we had moments ago were interrupted by another formation. What the hell do they want now? The company commander wanted to address us and congratulate us. He called us a unique band of brothers. He told us we would graduate and get our wings on Sunday afternoon. Saturday would be a day to turn in some equipment and square away our barracks. We would practice the graduation ceremony. Our commander told the graduates to shower and go to chow. He said the snack bar would be closed from six to eight p.m., except for us. The army provided beer. We could call home at the phone booths since our graduating class was the only soldiers at the snack bar. After three weeks of hard work, our instructors and cadre accepted us as airborne soldiers. I felt special and thought I belonged to a great group of guys. I went to chow and made it to the snack bar. The jukebox played songs that reminded me of being home and dancing with Christina. I was so proud that I had to call home.

I called home to my parents so they knew I had graduated from jump school. I called Chris, and I wondered if she would be home. It was a Friday, but still early, so I would catch her before she went out. She told me she was staying home for the evening and going to a show with her girlfriends on Saturday. I couldn't stay on the phone for a long conversation because other guys wanted to use the phone. I was so happy to hear her voice, and my heart renewed that she was still my girl. I returned to the snack bar to join my airborne brothers. We had some beers, and we sang along with the jukebox.

I got through Saturday, and I got my new assignment. I began advanced infantry training on Monday. I would be assigned to a weapons platoon. Sunday's graduation couldn't arrive quicker. The company wore its dress uniforms. We perfectly creased our pants and bloused them in our spit-shined boots. The company marched to the reviewing stand, and we stopped. The commandant of the 11th Air Assault Group would present each soldier with his wings. That was a special honor since the 11th Air Assault Group was created to test air mobility tactics. The program was deemed a success, and the army accepted the use of helicopters in combat. During the Korean War, helicopters performed medical evacuations and were used to scout an area. Now, helicopters were being used in a combat role, and the choppers had plenty of firepower.

A couple of years earlier, the 11th Air Assault Group formed at Ft. Benning. The group trained in Vietnam in an advisory role. It learned the best practices and tactics to use in a jungle environment. I didn't see the significance of getting our wings from the 11th Air Assault Commander. I would later understand what was occurring to us unsuspecting soldiers. But on graduation day, I knew I was among the best as they placed the silver wings on my chest. I saluted the officer. Then, I stood proud as my fellow airborne soldiers received their wings. I was no longer a leg.

The army had trained me well, and my eight weeks of basic training bonded me with 160 recruits in our company. We learned to do it the army way and felt the bond of being a team. During these last three weeks in jump school, I reinforced the army concept: one for all and all for one. Becoming airborne raised that feeling even higher. I had cared for these strangers. These strangers may have come from a different world and background than mine. But what we experienced together would last in my mind forever. Yet, the next day, I would move on again to another unit. I would meet a new set of strangers. I had no idea what would happen to all the guys I trained with, especially my airborne buddies. That would be a common theme in the military. The constant bonding only to move on.

IT'S WARMING UP

The weather had changed since early February when I arrived at Ft. Benning. The cold mornings and evenings gave way to a mild spring, and I had now earned my wings at jump school. My advanced training began in early May and would last until July. That training would be more infantry training, and I would qualify for other weapons. I had a lot of classroom training. I learned about the 50-caliber machine gun, mortars, grenade launchers, and light artillery. I also learned about camouflage and trained in cover and concealment tactics. I learned the art of flanking an enemy position and how to walk the point on patrol. My platoon engaged in field maneuvers against other platoons. I learned how to secure a perimeter and assault a high ridge. Physical training never lessened. Forced marches and mile runs were standard each week.

I had been away from home and Christina for four months. By the time this training ended, it would have been almost six months. I could ask for a weekend pass to fly home. But I felt the cost and the actual time I would be with Chris were not worth the heartache I would feel returning to base. I reasoned and was told I would get a week of leave at the end of training. My plan to get home after my AIT would have one more wrinkle. I was selected to attend a non-commissioned officer training course. I was chosen to be a leader in my platoon. This could add another rank above private. This course would begin one week immediately following my advanced training. I knew I would get a week of leave after the first week of July and have time to see family and friends. I couldn't wait to be with Christina.

During the last leg of my training, I became more aware of what was happening in Vietnam. Rumors persisted that several army units would merge at Fort Benning. Rumors eventually spread that the president would greatly increase troop numbers in Vietnam. Airborne units were said to be the first to arrive. During the Vietnam conflict, most of us thought the army was advising the South Vietnamese Army. To my knowledge, the Marines were the only US force in a combat role at that time.

During basic training and jump school, I and the other trainees focused on surviving. We had no contact with the outside world. But, during my last training phase, I had more free time. I could leave the company area and even get a pass to go to town. I didn't train on the weekends. I felt that all this training was excellent on my resume, and I had a great sense of accomplishment.

Meanwhile, I heard that our government was quietly adding more soldiers to Southeast Asia. Of course, these theories were rumors and opinions of us peons, so I didn't dwell on Vietnam. Besides, I had been brainwashed. Our government reported that the Marines were kicking ass. They said that with a few more troops, the communists would be driven out of South Vietnam. That all felt logical, and I trusted what our leaders told the public. The officers and commanders of these airborne units were eager to get into a battle before the conflict was over. The Pentagon and our President were painting an optimistic façade. They said that we were driving the enemy out of South Vietnam. Although we suffered minor casualties, we believed the enemy was being decimated. At least that was the feeling and the chatter at Ft. Benning. I could only react to the information I had at hand. It appeared to me that our airborne units, with all their weaponry, would demolish the enemy. So, if I had to go, it would be for a noble cause, and I would be fighting with the best-trained soldier.

I completed my advanced infantry training with a heavy weapons platoon and a one-week leadership course. My MOS (military occupational skill) was 11B, infantry. As promised, I was given seven days' leave after July 4, and then I would return to Fort Benning. Upon my return to Ft. Benning, I would be reassigned to a permanent company. I didn't care about reassignment. After six months, I was going home to the Bronx. I was going to be with my sweetheart, Christina.

I went home on leave and was proud to walk down the avenue in the old neighborhood. The wise guys were still sitting outside in front of Casa de Pepe, and they shook my hand. I spent every day and night with Christina. I reflected that I had grown up so fast since my last year in high school. I couldn't have been happier with the results.

My seven days at home flew by as I connected with most of the friends I grew up with on Belmont Avenue. I proudly walked on Arthur Ave., and everything looked the same. Chris and I went out with Roxy, her boyfriend, and the other guys and gals from the regular crew. Chris and I spent much time alone the last couple of days. Christina's parents and grandparents were very proud. They saw a guy who had worked on Wall Street and worked for Eastern Airlines while attending night school. Now, I am serving our country. They couldn't be prouder. They couldn't have been more naive and, like most hard-working blue-collar people back then, about the US involvement in Vietnam.

Vietnam started getting more attention after Johnson ordered the First Cavalry to Vietnam. Like many soldiers and the general public, people began to take notice of Vietnam. Like many people, I did not doubt that the US would end the conflict in Southeast Asia. I believed it would happen at little cost to American lives. The Marines were doing the dirty work. The First Cavalry, Air Force, and Navy would add the extra punch to defeat an overmatched enemy. The president's remarks influenced the thinking of many at the time.

As my last day of leave were upon me, I didn't think about Vietnam. My mind was filled with thoughts of Chris. During this last week, Chris and I discussed how this unexpected love affair between us seemed like we were meant to be. We still wanted to travel and explore the world, but we committed to each other to do everything together. At one point, even Roxy told me that she (Chris) loved me so much. Those words coming from Roxy meant a lot. She and her boyfriend had rocky times. During those times, they dated others. I interpreted her remarks as a bit of her own regret. She and her boyfriend didn't have the solid relationship that Chris and I possessed.

Although returning to Fort Benning was difficult, I was positive that Chris would wait for me. The first six months went fast, and I had 18 more months to serve after I returned to Fort Benning. The army paid for my round-trip flight, and I was flying out of LaGuardia Airport. It was an early flight, and I got to the airport early. My military training reinforced my early wake-up time. I had time to waste, so I walked to the Eastern Airlines ticket counter, hoping to see a former co-worker. I didn't see anyone I knew, but as I went to the gate, I walked onto the tarmac and saw many ground crew workers I had known. The uniform with my wings made an impression, and my old buddies wished me luck. I felt optimistic about everything that happened on a quick seven-day trip back to the Bronx. I was proud of myself. I appreciated all the kind words from friends, family, and former co-workers. I had just turned twenty while in the army and felt I could do anything. The most important thought in my mind was that Chris and I would be back together after I served my time in the army. There would be no more interference from the military. I didn't see what was about to occur.

THE FIRST CAVALRY

The idea of sending a significant airborne unit to end the Vietnam conflict made sense. Soldiers and our country believed in our president. At the time, no one could imagine that the next seven years would divide our nation.

This war would stain a generation of young men who served in Vietnam. Many years later, I would learn how the US buildup began. Before his untimely death, President Kennedy made subtle, quiet moves. They were not made public until some ten years after our involvement began.

I might go to Vietnam, but I might be reassigned elsewhere. If I went to Vietnam, I would go with airborne wings on my chest. I would be with a fighting force that would crush the North Vietnamese.

A week before my leave, on July 3, 1965, the First Cavalry Division colors were being returned and they were assigned to Fort Benning from its base in Korea. The 11th Air Assault Group and the 2nd Infantry Division were merged. They now fit under the umbrella of the First Cavalry. Other support battalions were also combined under the First Cavalry Division. The manpower authorization reached 16,000 soldiers. The units were made up of rifle companies and heavy weapons platoons. Over 300 helicopters and 1,500 ground vehicles were authorized for the new division. At Fort Rucker, Alabama, 200 aviators were trained to fly and use the weapons of the Huey Helicopter.

The airborne infantry was issued the M16 rifle. It was lighter than the M14, which had been the standard weapon used in basic training. On July 28, 1965, President Johnson ordered the Air Mobile Division to be sent to Vietnam. The airborne rushed a new class through jump school. Over 600 new paratroopers were airborne-qualified in a couple of weeks. Jump school training was cut from three weeks to ten days.

With all the emphasis of being airborne, there were not many jumps from planes or helicopters. Most airborne units jumped a couple of feet off a huey or landed in a landing zone. However, the air mobility to move troops was a great tactic, and the firepower from the Hueys earned the respect from the enemy who feared the sky soldiers.

In August, the first advanced detachment of the First Cavalry arrived in Vietnam. Troops arrived via transport ships, aircraft carriers, and air flights. Most units would be stationed in II and III Corps, which was located in the central highlands and further south toward Saigon, the capital city of South Vietnam. By the end of September, army engineers had completed an air base at An Khe. The base was located toward the coast, in the center of II Corps Vietnam. It would later be named Camp Radcliff for the first casualty of the newly formed division. On August 18, 1965, the first casualty of the new division was Major Radcliff. Major Radcliff flew a support mission for the Marines who had planned an assault and amphibious landing in Quang Tin province. At LZ (landing zone) Blue, the enemy waited for the helicopters to land with the Marine troops. The enemy opened fire as the Marines jumped off the helicopters. The Marines were taking heavy fire and casualties. Realizing the grave situation, Major Radcliff exposed his chopper to enemy fire. He provided suppressing fire as the enemy dug in on a ridge. The major saved many lives. He put himself in the enemy's direct fire so the troops could exit the Hueys and find cover.

By August, those 600 new airborne troops would have their fate sealed. They were rushed through jump school and assigned to the newly formed First Cavalry Division. They were also assigned to various airborne units throughout Vietnam. In hindsight, I went to advanced training after jump school. Then, I went to a leadership course. Because of the timing of my training, I was not assigned to the 11th Air Assault Group. The soldiers who had just completed jump school hopped over me. I was still assigned to a training brigade. Maybe I got lucky. I thought the army had forgotten about me, and maybe I would be part of the cadre in a training company at Fort Benning. I wasn't going on a transport ship with an airborne battalion or regiment.

REASSIGNMENT

July was half over when I returned to Fort Benning, GA. It was hot, and the red clay ground was dry and dusty when I arrived at the 3rd Army headquarters. I waited for my orders for reassignment to a new unit. I thought it would be within the First Cavalry Division. At the end of July 1965, the First Cavalry Division was ordered to Vietnam. I thought I was lucky because I was assigned to a training company for four months. I hadn't been assigned to any units that merged with the First Cavalry Division.

Around the second week of August, I received my orders for reassignment. I was assigned to the First Cavalry Division and would head to Vietnam in two weeks. I would get further orders and be assigned to a unit as a replacement when I arrived in the country. I was home on leave thirty days earlier, and the army granted me three days leave to return to the Bronx to say goodbye. The army booked my flight to JFK Airport in Queens, New York. It was an early flight arriving on the last Friday in August, and I called my friend Johnny and asked if he would pick me up. I didn't want to ask my dad or Christina because they were working. I would instead explain my circumstances at home and not over the phone. Johnny had no nine-to-five job; he was hanging around the bar and working for the wise guys.

Johnny picked me up at about 10 a.m. and drove me home to Belmont Ave. My mom was shocked to see me. She immediately called Dad at work and told him I was going to Vietnam. The first thing I wanted to do was to contact Chris, and after many questions from my mother, I called Chris at work. When I told her my news, the silence seemed deafening. It seemed the phone line had gone dead because Chris hadn't said anything. She asked how long I would be at home when the shock wore off. She said she couldn't stay on the phone, but her voice cracked when she told me. I wanted to end the call quickly, as this news was dramatic and upsetting. I told her not to worry and would pick her up after dinner when she was home.

I ate dinner with my family and told them everything I had to share. My dad was an infantry soldier during World War II. He was awarded two Purple Hearts and a Silver Star for gallantry in Italy. He was calm, and his advice was not to volunteer or try to be a hero. Just follow along with what the experienced guys did. I know he was trying to be brave for the family. My mom didn't say much except that I should write so she could write back and send me anything I needed. I gulped down my meal because it was Friday night, and I wanted to pick up Chris, go out, and have a good time.

After dinner, I called Chris and told her I would pick her up at about 8. She said she had called a few of our friends, and we would go to a few clubs in the Bronx. I arrived at Chris's house, and her mother gave me a big hug. Her father, who had served in WWII, shook my hand and said, "good luck, son." I was more emotional with her family than I was with my own. We didn't stay long. Being with Chris and the people I hung out with was a great temporary distraction.

On Saturday afternoon, Johnny called and told me to come to the bar. I didn't want to be disrespectful, so I agreed. The wise guys patted me on the back, bought me a few drinks, and told me to kick some ass. That evening, Chris and I went with Roxy and her boyfriend to Rockland County, just outside the Bronx. The nightclub had live music and a dance floor. Boy, it was great to go dancing, and when the band played a slow song, Chris and I held on to each other.

Dancing, we didn't say much, and I am sure her mind was racing like mine. After we left the nightclub, Roxy and her guy paid for a motel room where we shared a bottle of wine. Roxy was a wild card and always liked to party. She lit up a joint. I had smoked a joint a few times with RoRo and her Brooklyn friends. I had never shared it with Chris, and I didn't think she was into smoking pot. To my surprise, she took a couple of hits. We laughed and talked about how we all met, and Roxy told Chris and me to stay at the motel for as long as we liked. It was her present to us. Chris and I were alone and talked about the fact that we wouldn't see each other for an entire year.

We were so compatible, and we discussed all the adventures we could share when I was home permanently. We never discussed or implied that we wanted to marry. I was only twenty years old. I had a few intimate relationships and many dates, but I was past all that running around. I found someone who thought like me and was so easy to get along with that I just wanted to do everything with Chris. Chris felt the same, and she talked about all the "firsts" we could experience together.

After two days with friends, Chris and I decided Sunday would be our day to share. Of course, we had to have Sunday dinner with our families, usually at 2 p.m., which lasted a few hours. I ate dinner with my family and rang the doorbell at Christina's house by three o'clock. I would be saying goodbye to her family, and I hoped I would see them in a year when I returned from Nam. Chris and I were tired from the last two nights of music, dancing, and drinks. So, we decided to see a movie at the RKO Fordham on Fordham Road. In those days, it was a double feature. The RKO Fordham was a majestic theater; sometimes there were live performances. I forgot the names of the movies we saw, but I think one was a John Wayne western. What was playing on the screen didn't matter. It wasn't a Saturday night at the movies, but it didn't matter what picture we saw. We were hugging and holding hands in the balcony.

I dropped Chris off at her house around 10:30 and said goodnight. I didn't want to say goodbye because that sounded permanent. It was the most touching and challenging action I had ever experienced. Chris was shedding tears, and I could taste them when we kissed. She made me shed some tears, and while we were kissing, it felt like our faces were soaked in emotions. I waited for her to enter her house and drove away with misty eyes.

The following day, I was all business and had no more emotions or tears to expel. I had breakfast with my family, and my dad took the morning off and drove me to JFK Airport. I was in my Khakis, and my wings were prominently on my chest. I boarded a commercial flight. It would make a stop before reaching its destination in San Francisco. Another commercial flight took me to Hawaii. There, I would take a shuttle to the military airfield and board an army transport with other soldiers. My orders indicated that my destination was Nha Trang, Vietnam.

As the military plane approached the airfield, it traveled over the water. I realized that Vietnam had beaches. It was now September 1965. I do not recall when I arrived in Vietnam because the trip took so long with too many stops. I traveled through so many time zones, and the international dateline.

This trip seemed like a dream, and I was physically and mentally exhausted from my last weekend at home. All the emotions of the weekend and saying goodbyes to family and friends made my travels to Vietnam a blur.

When I landed, and the door opened on the airplane, the blazing sunlight had me squinting. I took three steps down the stairway, and the heat and humidity jolted my senses. I had been cooped up in a dark, air-conditioned airplane for a day. Now, I would face the reality of being in my new home. It had been like my past life was erased. I and the other soldiers were hustled onto a military bus. This bus had no air conditioning, and I arrived at the reception center for further orders. I immediately realized that the comfort of air conditioning would be absent for one year.

Air conditioning was a luxury growing up in the Bronx, and my home lacked air conditioning. As a kid, my dad brought home two box fans that he would put in the windows. I remember the fan had an intake and exhaust operation. My dad insisted on setting the fan on the exhaust option. His theory was to take the humid air out of the rooms. My sisters and I would rather have the air blowing on us. We would turn the dial to intake when Dad wasn't paying attention. To please everyone, my dad bought a couple of circulating fans. They could be placed on a table and moved from room to room. I didn't have to worry about fans now; I wasn't in my Bronx room.

I spent one night at the replacement center and was given my orders the next day. I was assigned to the 173rd Airborne Brigade, which was part of the 1st Cavalry Division. I was told to get on a truck and taken to a base camp near An Khe in the central highlands. It was a small convoy, and a military police unit escorted us. Several of the jeeps had M60 machine guns, and a quarter-ton truck had a 50-caliber machine gun. The trip took over an hour, and we made a stop for some reason about halfway through the journey. I discovered that the convoy waited because the road had to be cleared. We were about to enter a turn where the enemy had ambushed several trucks. I didn't know then that part of my daily function would be to clear roads and villages. This road was the main route to reach An Khe and Pleiku from the coastal port city of Quy Nhon.

I reached my assignment and was assigned to the 3rd platoon of my company. The company was not fully staffed with the typical four-forty-man platoons. I guess that's why I was a replacement. The first cavalry division was arriving via ships and the air. A division of 16,000 soldiers and equipment was not fully assembled until late September 1965. This was due to logistical challenges. My trip had been a whirlwind of stops, and I was glad I didn't travel on a ship. I didn't remember many of the units that patrolled the surrounding area of my base camp. The airmobile aspect of this war could have units criss-crossing over many miles. During World War II, regiments typically operated in one region and had objectives to take and hold territory. But Vietnam was different, and there was no objective of moving forward and taking and holding territory. The goals were to search for and destroy the enemy. I will learn so much in the coming months. But for now, I will take my dad's advice. He told me to watch the experienced guys and follow their lead. In Vietnam, many professional soldiers had only a month or two of experience, and most had no experience.

Luckily, my platoon sergeant was a career soldier. He had trained with the 11th Air Assault Group. The third platoon was a part rifle and part weapons platoon rolled into one. Surprisingly, I was given an M79 grenade launcher and my M16. Although my MOS, 11B, was basic infantry, I was qualified on heavier weapons from my AIT training.

Another surprise was reconnecting with a guy from my jump school class. George Lightfoot was in my jump school case, and George grew up on an Indian reservation in northern Florida. When he turned 18, he moved in with his older sister, who had left the reservation some years earlier. She became a teacher, lived in North Central Florida, and took George to her home. George had a hard time finding a job of any substance. He found the US Army to be his best option and joined. George was a big guy and carried the M60 machine gun. When George graduated from jump school, he had already finished his AIT. He was assigned to the 11th Air Assault Group, which was merged into the 1st Cavalry Division. George had been with the advanced party in Vietnam for two months.

It was great to have this connection with a guy with some experience. I remember George being at the top of our class in jump school. He had the features of an Indian and was proud of his heritage. The high cheekbones and bronze pigment in his skin set him apart from the rest of us. The guys in jump school broke his chops and asked how he got the name George. He told us probably after General George Armstrong Custer. Ironically, Custer was in the 7th Cavalry. The instructors called him Chief because he led the class in almost every category. The name stuck, and he preferred being called Chief instead of George. I didn't like my first name, so at least we had something in common. George had a keen sense of the land and sounds of the jungle and was a beast of a human specimen. He could play the role of an Indian warrior in a cowboy movie. I, on the other hand, knew nothing about the land. I could bop down Arthur Ave listening to Doo Wop on a transistor radio.

During my first month in Vietnam, my company patrolled around the area of Highway 19. The company provided security for convoys traveling from the coast up to Pleiku. We also patrolled hamlets and villages. We looked for the enemy or a stockpile of weapons and ammunition. We never found anything, yet the villages hid the truth about the enemy's whereabouts. The An Khe pass was along the highway, and the North Vietnamese Army ambushed US trucks and planted mines along this route. During that first month, I had not experienced any contact with the enemy, and we never found mines or stockpiles of weapons. We would revisit the same areas and get the same results. These missions were boring, but the anxiety and anticipation of being ambushed never left my mind.

By mid-October, our company had not engaged the enemy. We had not been on an operation that required boarding a Huey. That was about to change when my company received intelligence reports that a company of North Vietnamese regulars had attacked a village held by a Green Beret unit. The village was about 20 miles north of An Khe. The North Vietnamese Army was well-equipped, and it was also referred to as the People's Army of North Vietnam (PANV). Our enemy also included the local rebels (VC) who supported the PANV. The Viet Cong was the stereotype of the enemy wearing black pajamas. These local fighters knew the territory. They were adept at setting up ambushes and booby traps. They had an excellent knack for engaging a platoon and then disappear.

Two platoons from my company boarded several Hueys and headed to the landing zone less than a mile from the village. The chopper had two-door gunners, a pilot, and a co-pilot. In addition to the four-person crew, nine soldiers could be carried on the chopper. The 1st platoon would land and secure the LZ. My platoon would follow because we had heavy weapons. Then, a short time later, the third platoon would arrive after we secured the perimeter. I didn't know what to expect. I thought jump school was scary, but landing in an open field with no cover was even more anxiety-inducing than jumping out of an airplane.

The first and second platoons landed without incident. We received sniper rounds while securing the LZ and setting up a perimeter. As the third platoon landed, we received heavy enemy fire. We opened up where we thought the enemy rounds came from, but we couldn't see the enemy. So, as rookie combatants, our first encounter was nothing short of chaos and confusion. Our company commander, platoon leader, and sergeant had some experience. We followed their lead. Once the last platoon was on the ground, we searched for the enemy who ambushed the landing zone. The enemy had vanished, but we were looking for a fight. Our mission was to get to the Green Beret outpost and secure that area. We were sure that the enemy would attack the outpost again, so contact with the enemy and their retreat drew our company into pursuit. We did not want to break off contact, and their retreat was in the direction of the village, which was our mission. Our company was going to learn a lesson the hard way.

THE CHASE

To the best of my recollection, I am about to report what happened based on our company's action while we searched for the enemy. The short outburst of gunfire ended quickly, and the company thought it was probably an enemy security party to protect the rear of a larger NVA company. Our point man found a blood trail, but we didn't find a dead or wounded body. Our captain thought we should follow the general area of the blood path that would lead us to the enemy and engage and destroy the enemy. That became our mission, and we were less than a click away (a mile) from the Green Beret camp.

Our point man was moving relatively quickly, and he was hit with a sniper round. The next two soldiers' immediate reaction was to move forward. They wanted to provide cover for our wounded point man. We were on a trail, and the enemy had planted a booby trap that killed both soldiers as they moved forward. We would learn about the ingenious booby traps used by the enemy. This mine detonated when a soldier stepped on it. The pressure of the foot and body weight caused the detonation. It seemed to be a delayed reaction after stepping on the pressure plate. The mine was designed to explode when the soldier's foot pressure came off the trap. The explosion released pieces of metal upward, about three feet off the ground. You can imagine the types of wounds it afflicted on a group of soldiers. The soldiers called this trap "bouncing Betty." The projectiles seemed to bounce off the ground.

Luckily, the rest of the platoon had taken cover when we heard the sniper round. Those two soldiers never had a chance, and their lack of experience got them a ride home in a box. The NVA ambushed us, and nothing would bring those guys back from the dead. We didn't know how many enemies were engaged. We seemed to overpower them when the Chief set up his M60, and another soldier moved to a flanking position with his M60. My platoon Sgt. told me to send a couple of M79 rounds at a tree line. We could see the muzzle flashes of several enemies grouped together.

The M60s' suppressing firepower and a few M79 rounds ended the encounter. Thumper was a name given to the M79 because of its distinctive sound when fired. It could shoot up to 300 yards. I had two different 40-mm grenades at my disposal. A flechette grenade carried steel projectiles for close combat. The explosion created a beehive effect. It was designed to kill and wound as many enemies as possible. I used a flechette grenade in close quarters. The grenade inflicted severe wounds upon the enemy. We almost always used the flechette grenade. We were less than 100 yards apart from the enemy in most engagements.

Although the enemy retreated, we did pay the price. An RPG (rocket-propelled grenade) from the enemy wounded two of our guys. Lightfoot caught some shrapnel around his shoulder and arm. He didn't want to go back to the base camp. Lightfoot wanted the medics to patch him up. The chief wanted to stay with the platoon. I think I mentioned what a tough guy he was. The CO (Commanding Officer) was a Captain, and he radioed for a dust-off, which was a term used for a medical evacuation. It seemed that it only took a few minutes when I heard that incredible sound of Huey's rotary blades. Whomp, whomp, whomp! Huey coming to the rescue was the most beautiful sound for a soldier to hear under attack. I will never forget that sound. Whenever I heard a Huey sound, I knew soldiers were in trouble somewhere. Those magnificent iron birds in the sky did not provide a great deal of protection for its crew. The body of a Huey is made with a light metal frame. It had aluminum seating and plexiglass. Even today, when I hear a chopper, I look up and stand frozen in time, recalling a scene from Vietnam. When I think of the Huey, I can't tell you all the feelings that race through my head.

On my first day in a firefight, the body count scorecard showed one minor injury to Lightfoot. Two soldiers were seriously wounded, and we also lost two soldiers as a result of the booby trap. But the enemy retreated in haste and left behind ten dead soldiers. We found one wounded enemy soldier, and the medics took him back to base, and our intelligence unit would interview him. We knew that other enemy soldiers had been wounded, but the enemy was very good at removing their wounded comrades. The body count became the standard measurement of how successfully a battle ended. It always seemed that no matter our losses, the enemy would always have double or more of them killed.

My first day in battle was a blur, but while it was happening, I wasn't scared.

Everything seemed to be in slow motion, although it was noisy and chaotic. I was happy to be alive and not wounded when the smoke cleared. I felt terrible for a second about the two dead Americans. I didn't dwell on it because I didn't get to know them. Lightfoot returned two days later after his wounds were healed by the medics at our base camp. Our company had secured the Green Beret village.

Our company secured the village and brought medical supplies, and a few Green Beret replacements arrived via a couple of Hueys. We were given new orders and, after a few days, were airlifted further north into a more mountainous area. Our mission was to find and engage another enemy force attempting to take the high ground. Our intelligence concluded that several regiments of the NVA were in retreat. Several cavalry units took pursuit of the enemy. I did not know the gravity of the situation. After this first encounter with the enemy, our company had several days of contact with the NVA near Pleiku and other villages. I can't remember the names of these places. It did seem like the 1st Cavalry and various airborne units were in control and driving the enemy north. After the first battle in mid-October, casualties in our company became more frequent. This daily routine continued through early November. A dozen or so wounded were dusted off to a field hospital. The chief and I were still in one piece. After three weeks in the field, we went back to base camp for a rest, and then it was all hands on deck as the 7th Cavalry fought for their life.

IN DRANG

My first month in Vietnam was uneventful, and there was no contact with the enemy, but after my first taste of combat, my company engaged the enemy frequently. By early November, I had ridden the Huey to many different places. Sometimes, it was to join a fight. Other times, we searched an area looking for Charlie (enemy), and we slept under the stars for many nights. Well, if you can call that sleep, The Vietnam sky was beautiful and void of the smoke and smog that was in the Bronx. I could see stars at night. But the night belonged to Charlie (the enemy), and you could hear every sound in the boonies. The stars would be hidden if there were clouds, and nighttime became pitch black. That's when your ears, not your eyes, strained to identify sounds. The Chief was very good at moving in the darkness, but I needed a flashlight, which was not a good idea.

If the enemy were going to attack with a large NVA force, they would probe our position with small-arms fire. Lucky for me, my company did not face any nighttime battles. But, our frequency of engaging with and pursuing the NVA increased. We, for the most part, ruled the day because we had air mobility with the Huey Gunships. Platoons could arrive by air if a company needed help. My company went on several of these missions. We realized that our commanders planned to take the high ground, and once that was accomplished, the NVA would be driven out of the area. But with increased contact with the enemy, my company lost more men, and men were airlifted for medical attention.

All this action meant we would receive replacements. We had only been in the country for about six weeks and had fought for a couple of weeks, so I would be one of the old guys. Two of the replacements that showed up were Willie Patterson and Bobby Banks. Both guys had been in my basic training unit. Upon graduation, they went to advanced training. I went to jump school, and I guess at some point, they decided to go airborne. They had been assigned to the 1st Cavalry, hadn't everyone? Our company was never fully staffed with four platoons. With the loss of soldiers and over a dozen wounded who had not returned, we were hurting for replacements.

As mid-November approached, different units belonging to the 1st Cavalry took casualties. The casualties were due to increased contact with the enemy.

The US commanders were ambitiously pursuing a retreating enemy. The 7th Calvary suffered the most losses and wounded during mid-November at LZ Xray. The battle of Ia Drang pushed the 7th Cavalry to the brink of destruction. For five days in mid-November, the 1st and 2nd battalions of the 7th Cavalry fought a larger enemy force. The enemy force had two regiments. Our commanders rushed in pursuit to search for and destroy the enemy. The enemy had a significant advantage in manpower and held the upper ground. That had placed the 7th Cavalry Battalion in yet another well-planned ambush.

Many years later, in 1992, a book called "We Were Soldiers Once... And Young" depicted the horrific battle. The book told the story through the eyes of war correspondent Joseph Galloway. His first-hand experience and the events described by Lt. Colonel Hal Moore were not widely known by the American public until the book was published and a movie was made. Moore was the commander of the 1st Battalion, 7th Cavalry. The US claimed that over 200 men died and over 200 were wounded, accounting for half of the US soldiers. The US claimed the enemy had between 1000 and 1700 casualties. The PAVN claimed about 1200 were either killed or wounded. Both sides claimed victory.

The Huey saved the 7th Cavalry from the fate of General Custer at Little BigHorn. The Huey was used to attack the enemy and send reinforcements. They were also used to extract the wounded. The jets dropped napalm and bombs, and B52 bombers dropped their payload on the enemy.

At the time, I, like all of us soldiers, had no idea about the number of dead and wounded. We knew it was a life-or-death situation, and our airborne brothers needed our help. My company was dropped several miles away from LZ Xray and LZ Albany. The major battles occurred at these two landing zones. My company was sent toward the Cambodian border. We would intercept any fleeing PAVN soldiers trying to escape into Cambodia. The company set up a perimeter with another company, but we found no enemy. We dug in for four nights. Although we were several miles away, I could hear the B52s dropping their tonnage on Charlie.

It must have been late November when my unit finally returned to base camp at An Khe. I remember that because we would get a Thanksgiving turkey dinner with all the trimmings in a few days. After a week back at An Khe, my company did some security details on Highway 19. That was the same area where I had first entered the war. We had a few minor skirmishes with the VC but didn't sustain any casualties. A few more missions back to the area around Ia Drang did not produce any contact with the enemy. That was just as well; Christmas was coming, and it would be bittersweet. I thought the enemy took heavy losses. They didn't want any more fighting with the Sky Soldiers and all their air power.

Christmas produced a lot of care packages from home. We listened to Christmas music and thought about life at home. Some guys were married and even had babies back in the States. I had Christina in the Bronx and couldn't wait for her mail and Christmas cards. I didn't send a letter home because I was in the field in early December. I was moving to different locations in the boonies. By the time I got back to base, it was close to Christmas. The Post Office had to deliver many Christmas cards, and I didn't think my letter would reach Christina before Christmas. I did get letters from friends when I first got to Nam, but that frequency dropped. I could always count on my sisters and my mom to write. I appreciated the dry sausages they sent and the Ronzoni spaghetti and Ragu tomato sauce. Hey, it wasn't Sunday dinner, but it was enjoyed just the same.

I had time to think about Chris and wrote her several letters. My company did not have any overnight trips in the boonies or firefights around Christmas. I had plenty of time to remember Chris and couldn't wait to see her again.

1966

It was New Year's Eve. My company had been assigned to search for booby traps and the enemy along Highway 19. The assignment lasted from Christmas Day to the end of the month. We found no booby traps and no sign of the enemy. We had finished our mission and returned to camp in the late afternoon on New Year's Eve. We were going to celebrate the New Year with a bang. We anticipated that the next day would be free time. The juicers got loaded, and the heads could get high. Music would be on, and whoever had the reel-to-reel tape player was the most popular guy in the hootch area.

We had Motown and the Beatles newest music that played at home. Of course, there was also some excellent doo-wop. The southern boys loved their redneck songs. Their songs usually talked about a guy crying in his beer because Tammy cheated on him. At some point during my tour, I saw guys receiving that "Dear John" letter. Worse was a wife writing to her husband that she was leaving him. I saw soldiers break down and become solitary or risk-takers.

On New Year's Eve, I found a letter on my cot when I returned from the road. A mail call had happened while I was on the road, and there was a letter from Chris. The letter revealed that Roxy and Ronnie, her boyfriend, split up right before Christmas. Chris said Roxy, although hurt, would let her hair down in the New Year. Chris said the girls were going to a show and having a night out to celebrate the New Year. She told me that drugs were becoming an issue in the Bronx and that heroin had reared its ugly head. I knew that these issues had been underground for the most part, but the world was changing. Chris told me she was smoking pot more often because all her friends were doing it. Even so, Chris said she wasn't going to try anything else. Her letter spoke about how much she missed us being together. Chris reaffirmed that she would wait for my return. She wouldn't even want to go out on an innocent date. I felt very comfortable, and my mind felt at ease.

Like Chris, I was not into the drug scene, although I had smoked a few joints when people around me offered. I had smoked some pot since arriving in Vietnam, and tonight, the Chief and a few guys headed out to the secondary bunker line, which was not in operation. So, we sat there and smoked a joint, and then one of the guys had a joint dipped in opium. The Chief talked about smoking Peyote buttons when he lived on the reservation. I was feeling no pain when I floated back to the hootch. We never got high in the hootch or the company area or smoked in the boonies. It was always done secretly, but juicing it up in the company area was an accepted practice. Our New Year's Eve party released a lot of pressure off the guys. I felt good, but just like my last Christmas at home, the happy moments became bittersweet. My girl was half a world away. "My Girl" by the Temptations was universally accepted and played at every party. No girls were present, but black, hispanic, and white dudes sang with one voice. We held our imaginary girls before our eyes as we practiced the temptation shuffle. I Had many images in my mind of being home, but that night bonded the boys of Company B, 173rd Airborne.

As January 1966 ended, I had been in the army for one year and was starting my fifth month in Vietnam. Our company had minimal contact with the enemy in December. We had no casualties since November. Our platoon leader passed around information about R&R (rest and relaxation). It was a rest and relaxation week away from the war zone. It started after your sixth month in the country. All furloughs were five days, except if you went to Australia or Hawaii, you had seven days. I would have to wait my turn to pick my R&R week, as the list was in seniority order. I immediately decided I was taking the seven days. I wasn't sure if it would be Hawaii or Australia. I figured that I would never get this chance again to visit these places. I wanted to see round-eyed girls, and of course, I hoped that there was a chance that Christina could get some vacation time and meet me in Hawaii. It was closer for her than flying to Australia. I didn't have to decide until my turn came up sometime in February. I figured that my leave would be in late April or early May.

The war intensified, and by early February, my company had been airlifted in so many directions that I can't remember the details. We would get close to the Cambodian border, but we also humped in the southeast, moving closer to Saigon. The casualties that we had eluded since November hit us hard in February and March. The chief and I were still in one piece, but I lost two friends, Willie and Bobby, who were in my basic training unit. We lost others, and guys were wounded and sent to field hospitals. We never knew the status of the wounded guys unless they returned to the company. Did they survive?

Did they get sent home, or were they maimed for life?

The war weighed heavily on my mind, and I couldn't wait to take my R&R. I picked the last week of April in Hawaii as my R&R. I wrote to Christina and floated the idea of her coming out to see me. I didn't know if she could take off from work and night school. I thought she could use Roxy as a shield and claim that they were going on vacation together. Roxy would be up for that, as she had orchestrated the ski trips to Hunter Mountain in the Catskills.

My tour in Vietnam would end sometime in September, and I desperately wanted to see Chris in Hawaii. After my R&R, I would still have four months left in Vietnam, and I wondered if I could survive those last four months, especially since I hadn't gotten a scratch at this point.

I got a letter from Chris, and she said that Roxy was up for the caper and that she had a new boy toy that she would take to Hawaii. The snag for her would be getting off work. Roxy and Chris worked in the same department, and getting off at the same time might be difficult. Chris said that without Roxy as a shield, her parents probably wouldn't think it was a good idea for Chris to meet me. Chris said she could probably figure something out about missing some classes at night school. She said she'd get back to me about her vacation opportunity.

I understood, but I didn't give up hope. My main focus was staying alive and not getting wounded. I was getting the jitters; every day could be my last. The worst scenario was losing an arm or a leg. By my sixth month in combat, I had seen a lifetime of carnage. I told the chief if I was severely wounded, he should let me bleed out, especially if an arm or leg was missing or hanging on by a thread. That's pretty morbid, but that was my reality. Boy, did I need that R&R?

HAWAII

I waited for an answer from Chris about meeting me in Hawaii. But I had to pick my week so the army could schedule a flight and move on with their process. I decided to take the last week in April, and I wrote to Chris and told her the dates and the hotel I booked. About two weeks later, I received the bad news that although Chris could take a vacation, Roxy couldn't. The plan that she and Roxy were taking a break together went out the window. Chris said her parents gave her several reasons why she couldn't meet me. I knew meeting Chris was a long shot. Although it was discouraging news, I tried to reason that in less than five months, I would be home. Then, after another five months, my army service would be finished.

I had a bad feeling that I had to escape the war, and now I have that same feeling about Chris sitting home alone. Was it logical to think that a 21-year-old girl could resist the charms and passes of other guys? She was intelligent, smart, and a go-getter at work. I realized I had become too possessive. I wrote back to Chris and told her I understood. My letter was more matter-of-fact than the typical letters professing how much I missed her and couldn't wait for us to be together to explore the world.

Likewise, her recent letter took on the same matter-of-fact tone that she couldn't make the trip. Maybe subconsciously, I expected that the day would come when we would date other people. I truly understood that we had been together for about a year and a half, and at that time, I was away in the army. I think those one-week visits home from training kept the hope and fire burning. But now I will be gone for at least 12 months.

I received another letter from Chris before I left for my R&R. She said she wanted to explore Hawaii with me. She suggested that we could go there together someday. She told me to have a good time and heard that those Polynesian girls were tan and pretty. She told me to have a couple of dances but not to hold the girls too close. She said it was to be her job when I came home from Vietnam. Her letter was reassuring, and I wanted to relax and forget about the war. I thought that I shouldn't be thinking of what could have been if Chris had been with me on the trip. I was determined to have a good time and not sulk over her absence.

Hawaii was typically an R&R destination for husbands and wives to meet. It was a choice for a girlfriend and boyfriend to sneak away for a week together. That was my plan, but I was alone and on my own. Although I was alone, I made the right choice. Guys who went to other places told me to go to Hong Kong or Singapore. They said I could live in a villa, hire a girl to tend to my every need and have her escort me around the city. It was very inexpensive compared to a Hawaiian R&R. I could get a custom-tailored suit made in Hong Kong. I could have it shipped home for just a few dollars. All these were good points, but I didn't want to see any Asian-looking girls that would remind me of Vietnam. Besides, Chris would be on my mind, and paying a hooker for a week was not my appetite.

I wanted to be as far away from Southeast Asia as possible. I wanted things that made me feel like I was back in the USA. Hawaii was clean and uncongested, and it was very relaxed. The people were very nice. I tried surfing and discovered standing on a surfboard was much more complicated than it appeared. I rode on an outrigger canoe and visited the Pali Ali Lookout, which had a panoramic view of a valley with a rich history and folklore.

One evening, I walked over to the International Market Place. It had live music, bars, and restaurants. There were bayan trees and birds in cages, and I met some kids from California who were into surfing and searching for that perfect wave. They told me about these beautiful waterfalls at Waimea Valley on the north shore of Oahu. The valley was a sacred place and filled with folklore. I decided to take a tour and hike the trails. The waterfall was spectacular, and I thought of Chris and me exploring this peaceful paradise someday. My days went by quickly, and I spent many nights around the International Market Place. I met some girls from the University of Hawaii. All the girls came from various places on the US mainland. Most of the young ladies were from the western and central states. It was a new experience for me to meet women from anywhere other than New York City. The girls had never met anyone from the Bronx, so it made for good conversation. We danced together, and I displayed some of my rock and roll moves. I liked one gal in particular, and we had several slow dances. It had been about five months since I had held a girl dancing. She smelled so good and felt so good in my arms.

Despite missing Christina, I was having a great time, and the days went by too fast. In two days, I would leave that paradise and return to the heat, the bugs, and the bullets in Vietnam. I wouldn't have any great tales about sleeping with women. I wouldn't have any great tales about getting so drunk that I couldn't remember anything the next day. I had a great time, which refreshed my outlook on surviving Vietnam.

It was now May 1966. I had been promoted to corporal, and I was a squad leader. I had a few more months in Nam, and then I would see Chris. I would be out of the army by February 1967, which was only a couple of months after returning from Nam. On the flight back to An Khe, I dreamt of Chris and us going back to Hawaii. I would get my job at Eastern Airlines and perhaps get a good discount on a flight back to Hawaii.

As the plane approached the coast of central Vietnam, I got that same feeling I had the first time I landed in Southeast Asia. Seven days ago, I was back in the world. But the memories of those seven days in paradise disappeared when I walked off the plane. Heat and humidity caressed me, and no Hawaiian beauties were showering me with floral leis.

In a few hours, I was back at base camp with Company B. I settled into my hootch and cot. There was a letter on my foot locker that had arrived while I was away. It was from Chris. She wrote that she hoped I had a good time in Hawaii, and she understood if I hung out with some girls. She must have read my mind. Chris wrote that Roxy and her boyfriend had been given free tickets for a show to see Frankie Valli. A marketing guy for the Bronx Zoo, who knew Roxy, had given her two tickets. The zoo was one of the sponsors of the show. The guy said he was going and had an extra ticket. The seats were in a private box with a side view of the stage. Chris said she was offered the ticket but didn't know if she should accept it. It seemed that the guy could have given the ticket to anyone, but he asked Roxy to ask Chris if she wanted to go to the show.

By the time I read the letter, about three weeks had elapsed. I didn't know if Chris had accepted the invitation. So I wrote and told her I wouldn't mind if she went to see Frankie Valli. I told her I would go, especially since the seats were in a private box. I also wrote about the beauty of Hawaii. I wrote and told her we had to go there together when I was out of the army. I said she shouldn't sit at home on her hands. I wrote that we could do all so many things when I got home. I wrote and said it would be such a waste of time for her to do nothing because there was no guarantee that I would come home. The army and my actions in Vietnam showed me that anything could happen. It also taught me that changes were inevitable.

In May, my unit worked the coastal plains and sometimes the hills in the central highlands. It was getting warmer, and we experienced sporadic action. A few more guys were wounded, and the Hueys saved our asses a few times and got the wounded out. For some reason, I didn't write home or get a letter from Chris for a couple of weeks. When I finally got her letter, Chris wrote about her and Roxy going out in Rockland and Westchester Counties. She wrote that the Bronx was getting invested in drugs, especially heroin. Uppers and downers were becoming an everyday occurrence. Getting high in the workplace was becoming common at lunchtime. Chris was growing and experiencing new adventures, just like me. But, the experiences were in a different theater.

The heat and humidity increased in June, so I could count on being wet. When it rained, it poured, and sometimes it rained sideways. There were more insertions into some LZ, and more wounded brought us new replacements. My only buddy was Chief, and I didn't want to make new friends. I had lost two buddies from basic training, so I didn't want to go through that emotional roller coaster. One new baby-faced kid that I took a liking to was Danny Callahan from Rochester, NY. I was carrying an M60 because the last soldier to carry that machine gun was wounded. My platoon sergeant assigned Danny to carry the ammo for my machine gun. He would watch and learn the ropes from an experienced nine-month Vietnam soldier.

The weather had only gotten worse in July. I was short, a term describing how many days soldiers had left in Vietnam. By my count, I had less than 90 days to go. Danny now carried the M60, and I returned to carrying my Thumper, the M79. Danny spent about one month in Nam and held the machine gun for about ten days. Our platoon walked into an ambush. Danny set up his M60 to flank the NVA. The Chief set up in the center of our quickly formed perimeter. I was between them and sent some rounds from Thumper at the enemy. I heard someone yell rockets, and in a flash, the enemy fired an RPG at Danny's machine gun position. The kid had one month in Nam and was eliminated. That's how fast things changed. The RPG sprayed shrapnel, and I was grazed around my shoulder. I was dazed momentarily, but I could tell where the enemy position was, and I launched two rounds from my M79. The point man had been cut off as the enemy let him pass so they could ambush the main body of the platoon. It was furious for a few minutes. We lost Danny and three other guys.

The Huey gunships came to our rescue, and when the smoke cleared, we counted 22 dead enemies, and a few were wounded. From the original group of about 120 men in our company, we miraculously lost only about 29 guys. Some had minor wounds and returned after a few days at the base. Most of the guys who died were replacements, like Danny. I was pissed and wanted revenge.

I had enough of camping out with the bugs and snakes, and I was tired of being dirty, sweaty, and wet. I would hear that the temperature was 88, but with the humidity at about the same level, it felt like over 100 degrees. I wanted out of humping the boonies. The wound on my shoulder needed attention. They sent me back to base, but I knew I would go right back into the field. The medics saw minor scrapes from the RPG blast at the back of my neck. How that happened, I don't know. In any case, I would be at base camp for three days.

I NEED TO ESCAPE

I was back at base camp for a few days, recovering from some incidental shrapnel wounds. I had less than 60 days left in Vietnam and did not want to return to the boonies. The summer months in Nam were unbearable, especially for the grunts. Sometimes, we stayed in the field for two weeks before returning to base camp. After a few rest days, our company would ride the Huey into an LZ. Most of the time, the gooks let us land and set up an ambush as we moved into the jungle. That's what happened to Danny. I realized that most soldiers in Vietnam always returned to sleep on their cots each night. They got to eat in the mess hall and have a beer or two. A civilian would think those accommodations unacceptable. To a grunt, it was like having a room at the Hilton. The grunts didn't get to go back to a base camp every night.

The war was picking up, and while in base camp, there were notices about volunteering to be a door gunner. I guessed these brave guys were taking their lumps as they stood in the doorway of a Huey. I toyed with the idea of doing my last two months on a Huey so I could be in base every night.

I received a letter from Chris before being sent back to my company in the field. I had been writing a letter to her, explaining my wounds, and I intended to finish my letter before I left to join my company in the jungle. I didn't know how to explain my injuries. I didn't want to alarm her or make her worry. I didn't write home to my parents for that exact reason. I read her letter before finishing mine, and my heart sank. I had the same feeling the first time I jumped from a plane. As I read the first couple of lines, I felt like I had lost my breath. She told me about the concert and how great it was. After the show, she said, "Joey, the guy who gave her the tickets. invited her and Roxy to his apartment in Westchester after the concert. Christina smoked some grass and tried a quaalude, a downer, and they all fell out and spent the night there. She told me nothing had happened, but this was out of character for her.

Chris said it was so nice to visit places outside of the Bronx. She enjoyed visiting the suburbs of Westchester and Rockland counties. She even disclosed that, at some point, she could get an apartment outside the city limits. She told me she thought I should think about getting out of the Bronx when I exited the army. Her letter was missing the usual talk of us being back together and of experiencing all these things together.

Chris told me that Joey, Roxy, and her boyfriend had been going out together. My mind was blown because she said some guy had her attention. Her story was that they had been on several dates, but he was just a friend. I thought she told me the truth without being straightforward. In a previous letter, she said she didn't know the guy before he invited her to the concert. I was confused, and I started thinking the worst about Chris.

I'm a street guy from the Bronx. I've been on a few dates and relationships. I surmised the worst-case scenario. I had seen these signs of a girl or guy playing it both ways. When someone said, "We are just friends," it often meant they were friends with benefits. Relying on my street experience, I could remember how girl talk worked. I heard it too many times while in the company of girls. There was a way that a girl said she had slept with someone without being crude, like a guy. Listening to many conversations with girls, I knew the play on words. If a girl said, "I was going with him," it meant she had been dating. The length of the relationship didn't necessarily mean they had slept together. If a girl said, " I was with him," it often meant that they had slept together.

I dated a girl for a few weeks, and we discussed dating. She said she had only dated three guys. I had already known this girl's reputation and history. People have big mouths. I knew she had slept with three guys I knew. So she was telling the truth about having three relationships. She wanted to create the perception that she had sex with only three guys. Talks like this always made me weary of someone's honesty.

Perhaps I was overthinking her words in the letter. My fragile state of mind and being in a place where life had little value made me think the worst about my situation with Christina. On the one hand, I knew this could happen between us, and I understood to a degree. My mind was confused. I had less than 60 days left in Vietnam, but I had almost five months left in the army when I returned home. I had no idea where I would be stationed, and I couldn't bear to think of myself being home and not near Chris.

How could I compete with someone in civilian life? If I made it home, I wouldn't have an apartment, fancy car, or nice clothes. I was out of sync with people my age who might have an excellent-paying job and a nice apartment. I wouldn't have any of these things. The only thing I had was the experience of living like an animal. I watched people being killed or wounded, and I killed people. How could I compete with some scumbag that was interested in impressing girls to get in their pants? I was bitter! My airborne brothers and I were serving our country and following orders for our country, but the guys at home were partying.

I tore up the letter I had prepared for Chris and didn't write back to her. Instead, I inquired about volunteering for my last two months as a door gunner. I was pissed about losing the kid, Danny. I was pissed at the developments about Chris. I felt I needed to take out my frustrations on the enemy and could do that on Huey. I could save guys and come to their rescue. After going through everything I encountered since the first day of basic training, I felt I had little value. The latest punch to my gut was the letter from Chris. Someone had to pay for all my suffering. Someone had to pay because I lost the life I was living before being drafted.

I wrote to my friend Johnny, who took me to Sal, the jeweler. I asked if he had heard anything about Chris. At the same time, I went over to the aviation group, which needed door gunners. They would take me in a second because I had experience with the M60 and heavy weapons. The catch was that I would need to extend my time in Vietnam for another year. They would give me an extension bonus of $5,000. I wasn't sure at that point if I wanted to be away from Chris for another year. Undoubtedly, that would end my chance with her. But I was feeling relatively low. In retrospect, I was confused.

I felt like I was playing craps. When you play craps, it is very fast-paced. Sometimes, you just bet with your gut. I didn't think when I threw the dice at a wall. There was no plan, no strategy. You roll the dice, and whatever happens happens.

I put in the transfer request, but it had to be approved by my CO. If he approves my request for a transfer, I will sign the extension. I would be reassigned to an aviation unit where gunners were most needed. I could still back out of the request even if it were approved. I didn't think any of this out, and I was rolling the dice.

I was cleared to return to duty, and luckily, my company was returning from the field for a week of rest. On the last day before returning to the field, I got a letter from Johnny. He said he didn't want to be a rat on Chris and didn't want to trouble my mind about what he had heard about Chris. His letter described that Chris had been seen with some guys a few times. This was before the Frankie Valle concert. I didn't need to read more, and I felt like a fool. Chris seemed to be going out before I even wrote to her about Hawaii. So, I thought the whole episode about her going to Hawaii was a charade. She wasn't lying in her letters, but she purposely left out her true actions. The picture she portrayed of our relationship looked good, but her story about the concert was filled with disingenuous information.

That convinced me to sign the paper to accept a transfer and stay in Nam for another year. My captain granted the transfer. I never went back to the field as a grunt. It was with sadness that I would lose touch with the Chief, but he was going home in less than twenty days. He wasn't returning to the field. He was going home, and I was going someplace as a door gunner.

ROBIN HOODS

My orders came through quickly, and I was assigned to the 173rd Air Assault Group. I would be moving to Corps III. This area was south of the central highlands. I would be part of the 1st Aviation Brigade. The action in Corps III increased, and I went to a base camp called Phu Loi. Later, my company would move to Lai Khe. There had been heavy fighting in this area. It was called the Iron Triangle. This area in Corps III was located north of Saigon.

The Iron Triangle was about 120 square miles and had been a stronghold of the Viet Cong for many years. It was a vital area for the communists because the Saigon River and Highway 13 were important infiltration routes to the capital city, Saigon. The South Vietnamese Army made many attempts to control this area, but they couldn't drive the Viet Cong and NVA out of this important area.

The local villages were intimidated by the VC. The Viet Cong would kill the village chief if the hamlet sided with the South Vietnamese army. The American troops were learning the hard way about the tenacity of the VC. The US sent more soldiers into Corps III and more Huey's. More helicopters meant they needed more crews.

Rubber tree plantations and forests were to the west of the Saigon River. They were of vital economic importance. Hobo Woods was the scene of fierce fighting for control of the rubber trees and woods. Highway 13 and the Saigon River border the Iron Triangle, and at other points, Highway 13 ran through the heart of the Iron Triangle. Highway 13 was called Thunder Road because an aviation unit used Thunder as its call sign. There were four US fire support bases along the highway, stretching from Lai Khe in the north to Di An, which was further south. Highway 13 (Thunder Road) stretched north from Saigon. Lai Khe was about 35 miles north of Saigon and at the northern tip of the Iron Triangle. Lai Khe was named Rocket City because of the many daily rocket attacks directed at the base camp.

The provincial capital of Bin Duong Province was Phu Cong. It was close to the southern apex of the Iron Triangle. Phu Cong was about 15 miles east of the 25th Infantry base camp at Cu Chi. Cu Chi was within a few miles of

Cambodia and the Ho Chi Minh Trail. Di An was about 10 miles NE of Saigon and at the southern end, and the 1st Infantry base camp was located at Di An. Phu Loi was about ten miles from Di An and 25 miles north of Saigon. The 173rd Air Assault Group would support the 25th and 1st infantry operations. No wonder the 173rd needed replacement gunners. I would be in the thick of it.

I was assigned to Company B, and my crew chief was Specialist Five, Charlie Kenny. Charlie knew the Huey from head to toe, and I thought he could fly the thing if needed. He took me under his wing, and I learned much from him. Charlie came from the heartland of Nebraska. He was married, and other than sipping a couple of beers, he wasn't a party guy. He enlisted in the army when he was 18 and was now twenty-five. Charlie was shot down, his crew was wounded, and the pilot died. So, he extended his tour in Vietnam, as he felt it was his obligation not to leave his team. Charlie talked about leaving the military after his tenth year of service.

The pilot was James Smith from Houston, Texas. He was a career warrant officer, and from the first day I met him, I felt I was in safe hands. Mr. Smith was on his second tour. He had replaced the pilot that died on Charlie's Huey. A new co-pilot arrived in the company at the same time as me. Tom Patterson was from Erie, PA, and he was fresh out of training at Fort Rucker.

Phu Loi and later Lai Khe would be my home from September 66 to September 67 if I survived. It didn't take long to go on my first air assault as a door gunner. In September, I flew missions to support the 1st and 25th Infantry Divisions in Binh Duong Province. Those first missions were a new experience, and riding the Huey was exhilarating. If I compared jumping out of a plane versus riding with the doors open on a Huey suspended by a harness to the cabin wall, The Huey won hands down.

The military had colorful names for its operations. I remember names like Operation Atlantic City and Operation Tulsa. I remembered that our company might transport troops to an LZ. If our chopper had supplies, we would provide security and hover away from the LZ. After all the troops were dropped in the LZ, our helicopter would land and offload supplies and ammo.

The chopper that had dropped off the troops provided cover as we off loaded supplies.

My first two or three weeks of doing this were unremarkable, and we didn't fire a shot. It was sometime in October 1966 that my crew came under fire in an LZ. We were only a few miles from the Phu Loi base camp and west of Phu Cong. The 1st Infantry from Di An and the 25th from Cu Chi were on search-and-destroy missions. My Huey was covering the troops' landing, and the LZ immediately came under fire. We opened up our sixties. All hell broke loose as we touched the ground. Usually, Huey gunships provide the cover for the troops' landing. The gunships had their guns mounted and had rockets. Gunships could also carry troops, but the primary job of the gunships was to assault the enemy. As my Huey came under fire in the LZ as we dropped off troops, other Hueys swooped down and fired at the enemy in the tree line. We couldn't fire our 60s with all the chaos on the ground. We were very vulnerable on the floor of a rice paddy. The enemy had an excellent opportunity to cripple our chopper. We barely touched the grass, and our cargo of grunts quickly departed. As soon as we got back into the air, we had a better view and opened up with our 60s again.

That day was my first experience in combat as a door gunner. It was very different from being an infantry soldier on the ground. I felt safer on the Huey, except when we were on the ground. It would take several other missions before I got used to the sounds. The helmet I wore was much different from the steel pot the infantry used. The crew wore a helmet that had an intercom so that the unit could communicate. But it was hard to hear when the guns were firing. The sound of the rotor blade humming confused me, and the enemy's returning fire confused me. The crackling through my headset confused me due to all these sounds. After a while, I was able to separate the sounds. Communication with the pilots was essential, and that's what my ears tuned into. With experience, I could hear the crew's voices and block out the peripheral sounds. It became second nature for our team, and there was never yelling when we communicated. There was never a hint of panic in anyone's voice.

When my Huey landed back at our base in Phu Loi, the crew chief and I talked with our pilot and asked him if he noticed any problems with his controls. If there were no issues, we would look for any bullet holes from the enemy. Charlie Kenny knew every old bullet hole, and we didn't take on any new damage on the last mission. Charlie knew everything about our chopper. He and Warrant Officer Smith were shot down once. But this Huey, like many others, was resilient. After a mission, civilians may think the crew's job is over, and the mechanics will take care of the chopper. But the crew chief and gunner always spent time with the ground crew after a mission.

I was learning and watching Smithy and Charlie; our Huey was like a baby. We never walked away without reviewing any damage or mechanical issues we noticed. We would tell the ground crew what, if anything, was needed. We picked up the spent rounds and cleaned our guns. We ensured that everything was good to go if we received a call to rescue our troops. The maintenance guys on the ground were great. They felt personally responsible for every Huey that they worked on. That gave us an incredible feeling of camaraderie. After completing our mission, the best part was that I would get a good meal in the mess hall. I would not eat C rations out of a can and would have a few beers at the enlisted men's bar. I didn't have to sleep in the dark with the insects and be on edge waiting for a sneak attack by the VC.

In November and December 1966, we flew many missions in Binh Duong Province. We also supported operations around the air base at Bien Hoa. We received more fire at us every time we went into the air. By now, I had experience and could hear a round hitting us if it was on my side of the chopper. Through all the noises and the cracking intercom, I could distinguish that thud sound. At times, rounds would pass through the chopper and out the other side. By the grace of God, no one was hit.

After New Year's 1967, the war effort increased. We had three or two missions almost daily. I recall our unit supported a significant operation called Cedar Falls. We focused on supporting the 173rd Airborne Brigade in and around the Tay Ninh province. We dropped troops and provided cover along Highway 13, west of the Iron Triangle. This operation was coordinated with the 1st and 25th Infantry Divisions. The operation was our military's response to drive the VC and NVA out of the Iron Triangle. Our mission was to support the infantry units who were cutting off a fleeing enemy trying to find refuge in Cambodia and the mountains in Tay Ninh. I spent most of January and February 1967 flying missions in Tay Ninh Province. Whether you were a grunt or support troop, Tay Ninh was a lousy place to be on the ground. It wasn't a picnic flying into this area either.

Another major operation, named Junction City, would refocus and regroup the 173rd Airborne Brigade. It would also do the same for the 196th Light Infantry Division. They would fight a stubborn enemy in the mountains of Tay Ninh and as the enemy attempted to escape into Cambodia. The Ho Chi Minh Trail was along the corridor between Vietnam and Cambodia. The Ho Chi Minh Trail went south. The 25th Infantry Division base camp was at Cu Chi, near the Cambodian border. Extensive tunnels were used by the VC and NVA under Cu Chi. These tunnels had been there since the French-Indo wars. The tunnels were an infiltration point leading toward Saigon. Tunnels were under and near Phu Loi and Phu Cong.

The smaller guys in the infantry and the engineer units had the tough task of entering these tunnels. The enemy tunnels were an elaborate system to move troops and supplies into the south for their goal of taking control of the capital city of Saigon. The tunnels had places for the enemy to rest and get medical attention. Many tunnels were booby-trapped. Guys who went into the tunnels with only a flashlight and pistol were called tunnel rats. While I served in Corp. II with the infantry, I had no clue that tunnels existed. Corp. III was an exciting place.

Most soldiers, including me, did not realize that the tunnels were so close to two military base camps. It was no wonder that the NVA and VC fought with tenacity to maintain the Ho Chi Minh Trail and the Iron Triangle.

Our chopper took an RPG round on our tail sometime in April. Warrant Officers Smith and Paterson did an excellent job controlling the helicopter, but we were forced to make a very bumpy landing in a small clearing. We had just dropped soldiers and supplies at an LZ about a quarter mile away. The enemy was suspected in the area, but there was no contact in the LZ. Luckily, five other choppers provided cover while we were on the ground.

The pilots stabilized the tail, and we limped back to Phu Loi. The ground crew was amazed that we could control the helicopter and safely land. The damage was extensive, but that meant our team would get some long-deserved rest. Warrant Officer Smith gave us a free day and evening in Saigon. He told us we were to find some nice bar girls, and somehow he pulled some strings, and we had a room at a hotel. Charlie Kenny did not take advantage of the offer, but Tom Paterson and I wanted to take full advantage. I heard stories of the wild times at Saigon bars. Since Christina was only a memory, I decided that I needed some good love. Tom and I bonded. The unseen curtain between an enlisted man and his superior disappeared. We ate and had a steak dinner at the hotel. We went to a bar and had several young ladies climbing all over us. Tom went with one of the girls, and I went to a back room with another.

That would be the first time I had sex with anyone after my breakup with Chris. There wasn't any feeling except self-satisfaction. Tom and I had fun and made our way back to the hotel. I showered, and my head hit the clean pillow and sheets. I slept like a baby, thanks to Smithy and the cute bar girl. The adventure was short-lived, and I was back in Phu Loi the next day. I now had about four and a half months to serve my extended tour. At that point, I was ready to leave this war behind and return to the Bronx.

OH SHIT-I GOT HIT

After Tom and I returned from Saigon, our Huey still needed repairs. We had at least another day of rest before the work on our Huey was complete. While Tom and I were playing grab-ass in Saigon, our crew chief, Charlie, and our pilot, Officer James Smith, insisted on the repair. The command wanted us to take a different helicopter and send our Huey to the boneyard. The boneyard was the cemetery for the Huey.

Charlie and James had been on a couple of tours. Although the chopper had some holes and had been shot down about a year ago, they insisted on patching it up. They had lost a door gunner to enemy fire, and the co-pilot was promoted to take command of his own Huey. Warrant Officer Smith refused to give up on our Huey. There were too many emotional memories riding inside the Huey.

Our Huey was declared battle-ready. It was mid-May when our company was sent to Lai Khe. Another operation was being conducted in Binh Duong Province, and we would support the 25th and 1st Infantry Divisions. The operation would be located on the western and southern boundaries of the Iron Triangle. The infantry units were performing search-and-destroy operations. Our job was to either insert or extract troops. We also flew resupply missions and carried home a body bag at one point. This assignment felt more relaxed than the missions in Tay Ninh and near the Cambodian border. We had been in one fight, and May was drawing to a close.

Our crew was on a resupply mission with another Huey slick. A slick was the term used for a Huey, which only had two M60 machine guns. Our slick had Charlie on the left, and I sat or stood on the right side. A slick transported troops and supplies. A hog was the name for a gunship. There was more armament on board beside two machine guns. The Hog had rockets and a grenade launcher. The third type of Huey was used for a dust-off. It had no weapons and a big red cross painted on its side. It was used to carry out the wounded. The VC didn't follow the rules of the Geneva Convention, and a dust-off needed protection. Hogs flew in support of a dust-off, and a slick would join the fight to protect the unarmed dust-off.

On May 24, 1967, we were sent to resupply a company that had been in the field for a few days. A company from the 25th Infantry Division was working northwest of Phu Cong. Our Huey and another slick carried ammo, water, and rations to support the troops on the ground. We would land last, drop off our supplies, and then carry out a body bag. The intelligence did not indicate any large enemy forces in the area. The platoon on the ground had already cleared the location of the VC but had lost a guy to a sniper. The command decided to use two slicks to resupply the platoon, and the grunt platoon would search for the enemy for another few days. The other Huey landed first and dropped their payload on the ground. Two grunts ran from the tree line to retrieve the supplies. Another two grunts ran to the chopper after the first two guys were on their way back to the cover of the jungle. Things were well coordinated, and we stayed above, circling about 1000 feet away from the drop zone. My Huey touched the ground, and I helped unload the ammo crates and water cans. The last item to load was the body bag. Two soldiers carried the fallen soldier's body toward our chopper. The draft from the blades of the Huey created dust and noise. I was focused on pulling the body bag on board, and then our Huey was hit with a rocket-propelled grenade. I was knocked out of the Huey, and metal from our Huey and shrapnel rained on me and the two grunts on the ground. My ears were ringing, and I was disoriented. The two grunts lay motionless on the ground, and I struggled to clear my head.

I saw no enemy and heard our pilot ask for a radio check. But Charlie didn't respond. Tom, our co-pilot, said he had been hit. His voice was in pain, and he said, "Shit, I'm hit." He said he couldn't feel anything. I didn't hear Tom's voice again. I thought the worst and told James I was getting off the ground. At that moment, James said matter of factly, "Mikey, I got some bad guys running at my two o'clock." I got off the ground and used the Huey to hold me up. I looked toward the area off the right side of the Huey. I grabbed some mangled metal in the doorway as I needed support. My left leg was numb. Everything happened in a matter of seconds.

I saw three VC running toward the chopper. One had a bandolier, and the other carried an RPG launcher. A third enemy fired his AK-47 at my position. I heard the rounds hit the Huey, and I felt a sting on the upper part of my left shoulder. As the enemy emptied his magazine, I reached for my M14, which the explosion had dislodged. My rifle was in the doorway, and I grabbed it. The pilots all carried pistols, and I brought the M14 because it used the same ammo as the M60 machine gun. If the Huey went down, the extra weapons might be helpful, especially if we lost a machine gun.

God was with me because my M14 was at my fingertips. I picked up my rifle while the guy with the AK-47 was reloading. The three enemy soldiers were running toward us. I fired several rounds in their direction. I aimed at the guy with the AK because I knew he could disable me if he fired another twenty rounds. No one could have fired back at the enemy if that had happened. Our pilot could have been hit. Two of the enemies were kneeling on the ground. My instincts told me they would reload their rocket launcher and deliver a death blow to our Huey.

Remarkably, all these things happened in a matter of seconds. But my mind saw everything distinctly. The action occurred in less than 30 seconds. I was wounded and knocked out of the Huey, but I picked up the M14 right next to me. The M14 was semi-automatic, and I pulled the trigger quickly. I don't know how many times I pulled the trigger. I guess I got off about five rounds, and an enormous explosion happened. All three enemy soldiers were dead. They lay about 50 yards, or maybe closer to the Huey.

Warrant Officer Smith had the best view of what happened. The other Huey pilot above us saw the action. He dove his Huey down and raced in with guns blazing. Smithy wrote a report of the actions he had witnessed. The crew from the other Huey supported Smithy's testimony. To this day, I can't say if I hit the soldier who was reloading his weapon, or perhaps I had a lucky shot and struck the bandolier the enemy was carrying, igniting all the grenades. The other chopper was also firing their machine gun, so it was hard for me to say my shot was the death blow to the enemy.

When the three enemy soldiers were blown to pieces, I felt the debris and concussion of the explosion. I fell backward and tried to hold onto the back seat of our co-pilot, Tom. The back of the chair was covered in Tom's blood. Pieces of metal and plexiglass were stuck to his wet and mangled seat back. I collapsed in the doorway of the Huey. I drifted in and out of conscientiousness and remembered hearing voices, but I was in a dream world.

When my head cleared, a medic from the platoon we had come to resupply was directing others to tend to Tom. He was awake, and he kept saying shit. I saw them stuff some bandages on his back, and they left him in the seat. Then I heard the medic say that Charlie was alive but unconscious. A large chunk of his helmet was gone, and he was bleeding from his ear. The medic wrapped his head with a large bandage. Officer Smith was the only one miraculously unscathed. It was good because Smithy said he was flying our Huey back to base.

The medic saw all the shrapnel wounds on my left leg, and I began feeling the pain. I guess the rush of adrenaline had worn off. He gave me a shot of morphine, and I felt better. The soldiers strapped Charlie into the middle cabin, and I sat back in the well. The well is what was referred to as the door gunner's seat. The body bag that had been loaded on the Huey was on the floor of the center cabin with Charlie. A door gunner from the other Huey boarded since none of our crew could hold an M60. The two soldiers from the platoon who were wounded when the RPG hit our Huey were loaded onto the other Huey.

It had only taken a few minutes for all this carnage. A minute earlier, the two healthy soldiers brought us the body bag, but now, they were clinging to life. The healthy crew of four from our Huey would now fly back to base as three mangled bodies. I sat in my seat, nodding in and out of consciousness. I kept thinking that this mission had gone upside down in the blink of an eye. I kept looking at my torn and tattered uniform, especially my left pant leg. There were dark spots where the blood had soaked into the olive-drab flight suit. I felt a burning around my left shoulder, and my sleeve was ripped.

We would be in Phu Loi and the field hospital in a few minutes. Although we flew out of Lai Khe, we were closer to Phu Loi. I knew the doctors and medics would care of the precious cargo Smithy delivered. I remembered being lifted onto a stretcher and tossed on a table. My clothes were ripped off, and I couldn't care less. They gave me another shot of morphine as they searched my body for bullets or shrapnel. Hours later, I saw that a nurse was changing the bandages. The nurse used wet gauze to absorb the bleeding on several spots on my left leg.

I asked the nurse what had happened, and she told me I had wounds from my left foot to above my knee. Standing a few feet away, the doctor heard that I was awake. He gave me a more detailed report on the extent of my wounds. He told me my left pinky toe might not survive and I needed surgery. The injury above my left bicep resulted from a bullet that had grazed me, or the shot might have ricocheted off the Huey. I also had a piece of shrapnel removed below my belly button on the left side. He told me that the chicken plate I was wearing stopped this piece of metal from going deeper inside me. He told me not to worry; none of my vital equipment was damaged.

The body armor of helicopter crews differed from the heavy and bulky flak jackets issued to infantry and the other troops who didn't fly. The pilot's vests differed from those given to the gunners. The gunners had chest and back protection. These vests wouldn't stop an AK-47 round but might limit its damage. In this case, I think it saved me from a severe stomach wound. If the crew could get an extra vest or two, we would use it as a seat cushion. Enemy fire from below could rip through the bottom of the Huey and the aluminum seats used by the door gunners. Nobody wanted to be shot in the ass or, worse, in our privates.

I asked about Tom's condition. He was on a table a few feet away from me. The doctor said Tom, Charlie, and I needed to be sent to a Saigon hospital. He said that Charlie's prognosis was unclear. I was running a fever, and the doctor was worried about infection. He said we would all need further evaluation and surgery. The field hospital didn't have what we needed.

I wondered if the war was over for me. Maybe I would get a medical discharge from the army due to my wounds. I wondered if they would amputate my leg. But I was thinking too far ahead, and the next part of my journey would prove that I was in God's hands. Thinking and worrying about my future was stress that I didn't need. I was not in control, and the hands of the doctors and nurses, with guidance from God, were my salvation.

SAIGON

I was sent to the 3rd Army Surgical Hospital, which was located at Bien Hoa Air Force Base. The doctor and nurse at Phu Loi did an excellent job and removed all the shrapnel limited to the left side of my body. I needed surgery to remove my left pinky toe. My foot and my leg below the knee had the deepest wounds, and the left side of my foot was in poor shape. The doctors decided that the toe and the area on the outside near my pinky toe could not be saved. I had a wound above my ankle bone and a gash on the top of my foot. I had about a four-inch tear on the outside of my calf and a puncture almost behind my left knee.

Each time the nurse changed the bandages, I was sedated. The wet gauze had dried in the wound, causing pain when it was removed. I was awake, and their narcotic had me numb and high. I felt the pulling of the old gauze being removed and slight pain, but the drugs masked the pain. The doctor said it was a good sign that I felt discomfort. It meant that the nerves were alive. If the area died, they would have to cut that area off. That's what happened to my toe and a sliver on the side of my foot. The doctors were concerned that if they didn't remove the dead toe and tissues, an infection could spread.

I was scheduled for surgery, and they gave me a numbing agent. Then I felt nothing below the waist, but I heard the sound of the saw that removed the toe and dead tissue. The surgeon waited a few days to ensure the infection subsided and that I did not need further cutting and trimming. I lost track of time, but the surgical team would take a patch of good skin from my thigh. They would use the skin and graft it around where they did the amputation. I was frustrated because I wasn't allowed to walk on the graph. I was wounded on May 24th, but it was mid-June, and I had not been out of bed.

My wounds were healing, but they needed to be packed with gauze and changed twice daily. I enjoyed the medication because it relaxed me and made me feel no pain. I'd usually get the dressing changed after dinner and around 6 a.m. The injection would arrive about 20 minutes before the doctor looked at the wound. But one morning, the doctor showed up before I got my shot. He told me not to worry and didn't want me to take the pain-killing narcotic. The wet gauze had dried, and the doctor yanked it out of my wound. The hole was closing from the gaping slit I had when I was first wounded.

I grabbed the nurse's hand and screamed. The doctor said my reaction was good, and my leg was alive. There was no sign of infection. He told me I would be moved and start some rehab. I would be shown how to care for my wound.

It was the last few days of June, and I found myself in the 3rd Army Hospital in Saigon. I wondered if the army would send me home after the rehab. I was to go home in September, as my commitment to extend for one year in Nam would end. I was in the hospital for another three weeks. I met a nurse who cared for me and a dozen other soldiers. Her name was Gina. She was 26 and from Brooklyn, NY. She lived close to the neighborhood where Rosalie lived. I immediately took a liking to her. She was so caring toward us guys. She turned me on to some weed when she took me outside for therapy. After her shift ended, she would take me out of the hospital ward. The hospital ward was a hut with about ten beds on each side of this long room. Every bed was filled. There were guys with wounds that were much more serious than mine. I saw guys with missing limbs or disfigured faces.

She always asked if I was in pain and gave me some pills that made me feel mellow. She had great compassion and was like the pusher man delivering drugs to us soldiers. Eating some narcotics and smoking grass became a daily habit. I wondered what in her background would make her come to Nam. She jeopardized her career by handing out pills and weed like it's candy. I didn't care; I only wanted to go home and say goodbye to the army. I tried to forget the scenes of May 24th. For the first time, I questioned if all the fighting was worth it. I hoped I would go home and be discharged in a few weeks.

It was sweltering and humid in July, and I would sweat while lying in bed. All the drugs Gina provided, both prescribed and illicit, only made me sweat more. At the end of July, a doctor and another nurse talked to me about how I would feel if I were discharged and sent back to my unit. They asked if I could tend to my wound and keep it clean. I immediately put up my defenses. I asked myself if these people were kidding or just stupid. I talked silently and questioned if they knew the awful conditions I would be in if I was sent back into the field. I asked them what I would be doing. They said they would place me on restricted duty and limit my walking. I wouldn't be going outside the perimeter.

I thought the army was screwed up. I questioned why they wouldn't just send me home. What practical use would I have back in my unit? They said it wasn't up to them to send me home. They said they could recommend another company in Long Binh, Vietnam's most extensive military base. It was the home of over a thousand soldiers and the central supply depot. I thought for about 30 seconds, but I said, "No!" I wouldn't go through the trouble of meeting new guys for another two months. I told the doctor to send me back to my unit. I wanted to go back because I had my personal belongings there. I also wanted to thank Warrant Officer Smith.

The next day, I received my orders. Gina was the one who gave me the news. She helped me pack and gave me dressings and bandages to keep my wound clean. She also gave me a stash of pills for the pain. It was precisely two months after I was wounded, and I would get a ride to Bien Hoa Air Base. There, I hopped on board a chopper and flew back to Phu Loi. I was going back to the 173rd Airborne Brigade.

I had grown very fond of Gina, and although I was happy to leave the hospital, I was despondent. I felt that I was losing the only friend that cared about me. I gave her my address in the Bronx. I secretly hoped I could get together with her back in New York. She said when she came home, she would look me up. But she said I would probably have a few girlfriends when she arrived home. She gave me a cane to support my left leg and ease the pressure on the skin. We hugged, and I kissed her on her cheek, and she reciprocated. I got choked up with emotion. My eyes welled up. I had to move out quickly; otherwise, I would have made a scene crying.

PROMOTION

I arrived at my unit and returned to my hootch, and my foot locker was still there. A rubber band holding a couple of letters from home was on my cot. A new guy occupied Charlie Kenny's cot. Several new guys had taken over the spaces of guys I had lived with for over half a year. It had only been two months since I was gone, but I felt the world had changed. My only world now was this eight-man hootch, but I felt like a stranger. Bobby and Rick were the two-door gunners on the Huey that had accompanied our chopper on the day I was wounded, and they were still in the hootch.

I was happy to see them, and they were surprised to see me. I asked if they knew what had happened to Charlie. They said Officer Smith had kept tabs on my crew. Smithy told them that Charlie had been sent back to the States. He needs specialized rehab for the head wound he sustained. I was told that co-pilot Tom returned a few weeks ago and got promoted. Thomas Patterson would now be in charge of his crew. Mr. Smith had a new Huey and team. Smithy had left an envelope for me, and it was with the letters from home. I didn't want to do any more walking on my feet. It had been a long and emotional day. I remembered that Gina told me to take it easy on the leg.

It was time for chow, and I had to make one more walk to the mess hall. I didn't have time to open my mail. I was starving, and the food in the hospital wasn't good. With my cane in hand, I limped to the mess hall and ate with Bobby and Rick. Several other guys came by to welcome me back. A couple of guys from the maintenance crew and a clerk were familiar faces. After eating, I just wanted to get to my cot and read my mail. I didn't want to shower because I was very tentative about my injured foot. After chow, I returned to my hootch, got water, changed my bandage, and cleaned my foot.

I read the first couple of letters from my family. I felt terrible because I had not written to them in over two months. I never told them about being wounded. As I was reading my mail, Officer Smith walked into the hootch. We embraced, and he welcomed me back to the Robin Hoods. Smithy told me that his obligation was to notify the families when a crew member was wounded. Smithy wrote to Charlie's wife, my parents, and Tom's family.

I didn't know this, but Charlie would have rotated out of the country on June

30th. Charlie was finishing his second tour but never let on that he would be leaving that soon. Smithy knew this, and sometime in April, he put in the paperwork for me to replace Charlie as crew chief. Smithy set it up so I could get promoted to Specialist E-5. The company organizational table had an E-5 crew chief and the door gunner as an E-4. While in the hospital, I was officially promoted to E-5 crew chief on June 30th. Mister was the proper way to address a warrant officer. Huey pilots and co-pilots were warrant officers. Their rank wasn't equal to an officer's. They were between a non-commissioned officer (Sgt) and a second LT. Mister was technically the proper term to address warrant officers. As time passed, Mr Smith told me to address him as Smithy in our crew circle. Out of respect, we always referred to Mr. Smith if we were talking about him with anyone outside our crew.

To me, Mr. Smith was respected as a person, a Huey pilot, and a family member. He looked out for his crew. I found the orders for my promotion with the letters on my cot. He told me he wasn't sure if I would be back to fly as his crew chief. But he wanted me to be promoted even if I would not return as a crew member. Like Charlie, Mr. Smith was on his second tour, and I didn't know much about his personal life. He had some pull with our commander and got my promotion expedited.

I think I said thank you a dozen times. I was at the end of my second tour, although I had not been a door gunner for the entire time. My second tour would be over in mid-September. Smithy told me he might extend for another year. I thought he was crazy. It seemed to me that Smithy was pushing his luck. He said I saved his life and the lives of the other crew members when I eliminated the second RPG from being fired. I said it was a lucky shot. We talked for a while, and I was emphatic that I wanted to go home and finish my last four months in a support unit. I wanted my wounds to heal completely, and I didn't need to go to some gung-ho airborne division.

Mister Smith said he understood. He told me he would try to get me to a transportation or supply company for my last two months in Nam. I spent the next three weeks doing little and worked in the maintenance shop, pushing requisitions and storing parts. I was told I was reassigned to a company in the 610 Maintenance Battalion. On the day I was set to leave the Robin Hoods, I was told to report to headquarters. It was an emotional day, and I had many memories of the guys I had met. The previous night, I had a few rums and cokes, and the guys said their goodbyes.

It was early the following morning, and I had packed all my gear and personal effects the night before. My duffle bag was filled with the two uniforms I wore as an airborne infantry soldier. I took my cutoffs, a bathing suit I bought in Hawaii, and civilian shirts. With my cane and the duffle bag swung over my right shoulder, I went to the headquarters building. There was a jeep outside that would give me a ride to my new unit. My new home was only two companies away from the Robin Hoods. Jeff, one of the company clerks, would drive me to the new company. He told me to go inside and sign out. I entered the building and more than the usual number of soldiers were inside. I recognized their faces, and Mr. Smith tapped me on the back and directed me to the commander's rear office.

I was surprised that Smithy was there with all these other guys. I had just shared some drinks with them the previous night. The commandant was sitting in his chair behind a desk at the rear of the building. Mr. Smith escorted me to the back of the room, and the commander stood and came around the front of his desk. The First Sgt yelled attention, and those in the room snapped to attention. Smithy turned me around to face the seven or more soldiers in the room. I saw Tom, some gunners, and a crew chief from other Huey's in my company. There were also a couple of maintenance guys who I knew well.

The company commander read the award which I was about to receive. Mr. Smith wrote and described the action he witnessed on May 24, 1967, in Binh Duong Province, Republic of South Vietnam. The award stated that Specialist 4th Class Francis M. Di Natale disregarded his wounds and placed himself in direct sight of three enemy soldiers.

The enemy fired a rocket-propelled grenade that disabled most of the crew and soldiers on the ground when an RPG hit the Huey. Disregarding his safety, specialist four, DiNatale, exposed himself to the enemy. He killed the three enemy soldiers with his M-14 as the enemy prepared to fire another

RPG at the helpless Huey. Specialist Di Natale's brave and heroic action inspired all who saw it. It exemplified the heroic qualities of the men of the 173rd Air Assault Brigade.

The commander shook my hand and ordered those in attendance to be at ease. There was applause and shouts of "Airborne" as I stood there frozen. Then it got quiet, and there was an awkward pause, so I thought I should thank the commander out of respect. I thanked the commander and added a few heartfelt words about Mr. Smith. Smithy once again displayed his leadership by caring for me. He did so in his efforts to have the army approve this award. I received a Bronze Star with Valor. I also received a purple heart. I told those in attendance that from the first day I met Mr. Smith, he always put the needs of his crew first. I thanked Smithy for writing to the families when all three of his crew were wounded. I described how many times Mr. Smith steered our Huey to aid troops on the ground. I pointed out that his action saved many soldiers on the ground.

I began to choke up, so I stopped talking. Everyone shook hands with me, and there were hugs all around. I shook Smitty's hand and told him I knew he had my address in the Bronx and hoped he would write. I told him I would ask my mom to send him some care packages. Everyone had a mission or job, so everyone went on their way after a few minutes. Jeff, my driver, said, "Let's go," and off we went. There wasn't any conversation on the 5-minute drive to my new unit. During the five-minute drive, I wondered how the army creates excellent relationships and camaraderie, but the very nature of the military and war causes losses and changes, so nothing stays the same.

I thought it was ironic that all the changes I went through in the army mirrored all the changes I had from Rosalie to Christina. Nothing stays the same! My heart was tossed up and down. All that I experienced in the army, from jump school to being a door gunner, made me numb. The war had ripped at my heart. I knew one thing: I would be safe and happy only when I went home and put the army behind me.

IT'S NEVER OVER

It was a great send-off from the guys at the 173rd Airborne Brigade. I was so proud of all those guys, particularly Mr. Smith, Tom, and Charlie. Everyone who served in the Huey Company was vital to winning battles. The risks and sacrifices of the boys flying over the treetops didn't matter. Their only purpose was to rescue a fire support base under attack or save an infantry company from being overrun.

The crews were shot down, or sometimes they crashed due to mechanical failure. But they got back into the sky without hesitation. Many of these soldiers never got the chance to fly again. My thoughts also brought back memories of walking on patrol with the chief and the boys in my infantry unit. I lost friends and was completely frustrated walking around the jungle and living like an animal. It made me wonder if the war was worth the sacrifice. Even though I was wounded as a door gunner, I reasoned that I made the right decision to get out of the infantry.

I could have sucked it up and finished my last two months in the infantry unit. I could have gone home and finished my service in five months. I chose to stay because I felt it was my duty to the guys who had given their lives. Furthermore, I thought I couldn't go home and face the fact that Chris and I were done. I had to convince my mind that I made the right decision, but it wasn't easy.

To this day, I replay my decisions and try to understand my motives from over fifty years ago. I wonder, and play what if I did this or that game? I conclude that my heart endured a journey that most can't fathom. I made decisions based on the information I had. But, my emotional health influenced my need to be part of something special. At that time, I didn't feel great about myself. Christina's thoughts had kept me going. I have great memories of the scenes on Belmont and Arthur Avenues. In my mind, I could see wise guys on the corner or the smell of the subway and memories of walking to my grandstand seats in Yankee Stadium. These images were vivid reminders of a life I left behind. I wanted to return to 1964, but that seemed so far from my reality. I thought of all the instances of doing those things with Christina. Now all I had was my airborne brotherhood. My companions were the M-60s, diving from the sky to the treetops with blazing machine guns. I kept thinking about all these things the last night I spent with the Robin Hoods. These thoughts kept sneaking into my mind as I got medals pinned on my chest. These thoughts accompanied my ride to my new company in Nam.

I quickly said goodbye to Jeff when I arrived at the 610th Maintenance Battalion. As he drove off, I felt I would have to say goodbye to all those thoughts of being part of the 173rd Airborne Brigade. I felt that I had done my duty. I went inside the battalion headquarters, and the clerk gave me orders. I finished my last few weeks working with the 758th Service and Supply Company. The clerk saw my record as well as the First Sgt. The First Sgt walked me to my hootch. I would sleep in my last hootch for a few weeks before my orders to leave Vietnam arrived.

I met a few guys inside the hootch, and it looked the same as every hootch I had called home. The First Sgt told the guys in the hootch to show me the ropes. I would report to the warehouse in the morning. I didn't do much work, and no one seemed to care if I did anything. I didn't get friendly with anyone. I didn't have conversations about where you came from or when you were going home.

I know the shoulder insignia patch of the 173rd Airborne let everyone know that I had been in the shit. That was the terminology for combat. I'm sure the guys saw my wounds and bandaged foot when I showered. These guys gave me a wide berth to do whatever I wanted. My last few weeks couldn't go fast enough. I watched some movies in the evening if they had a movie night. I had a few drinks at night and ate some of the painkillers that Gina had given me. I was enjoying the concoction of a pill and alcohol.

Finally, I received my orders to go home. The soldiers in my temporary home were good guys. They were staying, and I was returning to the world. I was anxious on the day I was leaving Nam. I had to take my last ride on Highway 13. I was wearing my khakis and had all my patches and ribbons displayed. My boots were standard stateside boots, not jungle boots. My pants were bloused properly. Mama Son had pressed and starched my uniform. I gave her some MPCs, military payment certificates, instead of piasters, Vietnam currency. She was very grateful.

As I took my last ride down Highway 13, I hoped it would be without incident. That road traversed through the Iron Triangle. So, coming out of Phu Loi, our three-jeep caravan could be vulnerable. After traveling south for ten miles, the probability of an ambush diminished. The out-processing center was located a few miles from Saigon and the airport. I would get my ticket stamped and receive orders to report to the next army base. I would shuttle to Tan Son Nuet Air Force Base and take a commercial flight to the USA.

I arrived at Tan Son Nuet and got in line with the other lucky guys going home. There was no cheering or laughter. We all anticipated what was happening, but nobody wanted to put a jinx on us because it wasn't over. It wasn't over until the wheels of that big, beautiful Pan American jet lifted off the ground. Only then would this nightmare be over. We weren't safe until we got into the sky. At least, that's what I perceived.

My mood lightened as I entered the plane's cabin, where a pretty stewardess welcomed us. I went to my seat. These angels in blue Pan Am uniforms and pillbox hats checked our seat belts as they walked up the aisles. The lead stewardess got on the intercom and welcomed us home. She said it was an honor for the crew to take us home. That made me feel good.

The plane began to taxi, and I heard the captain tell the crew to get ready for takeoff. I could feel the vibration of the engines and listen to their roar. The plane moved down the runway, and I waited to not feel the tires on the ground anymore. I think everyone had the same thought because a tremendous roar filled the cabin as we got off the ground. Everyone was cheering and clapping.

In less than a minute, we could see the coastline. The captain came on the intercom and said he would gladly take us home. He told us we would stop in Guam and continue to our final destination in San Francisco, California. It was over.

WELCOME HOME

It was a long flight to Guam, and I don't remember much about the journey. I slept on and off until the plane landed and refueled in Guam. I then had to deplane with the other troops. It was hot outside, much like the temperatures in Nam. But, there was a nice breeze and no danger of a rocket attack. The best part of getting off the plane was going inside the terminal. It had air conditioning. There was also a bar, and we crowded around it.

We converted our MPC to greenbacks when we were processed out of the country. I had about 100 bucks, which I accumulated over time in Nam. The drinks were cheap, and I still had the pills Gina had given me. I thought about her and that she was still in Nam. She gave me about thirty pills when I left her care. I didn't use the pills until I got to the maintenance company. I regularly took a pill that Gina had given me for pain while drinking alcohol.

I went to the men's room to sneak a pill. Then I went back to the bar and had a drink. I felt relaxed. Most of the conversations around the bar were about what each guy would do when he got home. Most guys couldn't wait to go to clubs and bars and hook up with a girl. I had been away from civilian life since January 1965, when I joined the army. I would return to the world after spending two years in Vietnam. My service would be complete about four months after returning from Vietnam.

I knew Christina would be a distant memory, but I was ready, willing, and able to pursue as many women as possible. I couldn't wait to walk down Arthur Ave or to watch a baseball game at Yankee Stadium. Of course, seeing my family would be comforting. I knew my mom would feed me, and I could taste the spaghetti and meatballs. I remembered the smells and the aroma of the gravy cooking on our stove every Sunday morning. No longer would I top my spaghetti with Ragu meat sauce. I could go to the greasy spoon diner and eat a charbroiled, juicy cheeseburger. I would sleep in my old room in a real bed. I could listen to the radio and all the new hit songs. All these things were on my mind as I waited to return to the States.

An announcement came over the loudspeaker advising us to proceed to the gate for boarding on our Freedom Bird. I felt excited as I went to the gate and up the stairs to the jet plane. I couldn't wait to land on US soil. I talked a bit on the flight with the guy on either side of me. I wondered how great it would be to be away from the war. I slept for most of the trip.

When I woke up, the stewardess was talking to the guys in my row, and she asked if I needed a blanket. The three stewardesses were so friendly to us. I wondered how many more hours of flying time I had left. I asked the stewardess, and she said in about an hour we would land at Oakland International Airport. That news kept me up, and I had slept a lot, so I kept looking out the plane's window. I was looking for the lights on the shoreline of California.

The pilot came on the intercom and said to look out the aircraft's left side. He said that in a few minutes, we would see the California coast. Everyone's eyes strained to view the coast of California. My eyes strained as they did while I sat in the dark in the jungle. It didn't take long, and we all saw some lights faintly in the distance. As we got closer, I could feel the excitement of the other soldiers on the plane. The captain returned to the intercom and said, "Gentlemen, there it is."

The captain said we would start our descent to the Oakland airport. He said, "I know you have been waiting to get home, and it has been my pleasure and honor to take you home." The flight attendants came down the aisle to check our seat belts. They shook our hands, and some guys held their arms while tears blinded them. That was emotional, and it's hard to explain. It was a moment that only those there could understand. It was an unspoken bond between strangers. Yet the crew and guys who, 24 hours earlier, had met for the first time felt like we had been lifelong friends.

We could see the airport, and like all the missions we had been on in Vietnam, there was anticipation and silence. Then, I felt the landing gear being lowered. I could see the runway as the jet finally approached the glide path. I held my breath like everyone else, and we were about a couple of hundred feet from the runway. In seconds, I felt the wheels hit the runway, and the thrusters from the jet's engine helped slow the plane. Someone clapped, and then others clapped. Then the soldiers erupted into a roar. As we taxied to the gate, the stewardess came on the intercom and welcomed us home.

The plane stopped, and the engines were turned off. We would stand up and make an orderly exit. As we passed the three flight attendants, the captain, and his crew, they shook our hands. Some of us got a hug from these lovely ladies. "Welcome Home" has been said and used many years after the fact. This is because Vietnam veterans were never accepted or appreciated by our government. US soldiers were never welcomed home by many in public. Even our peers didn't care about me and my brothers.

But, on the day I landed back in the world, these seven strangers welcomed us with open arms. I believed their sincere words and actions toward me and my fellow soldiers. I thought I would experience that when I returned to the Bronx. Forty-eight hours earlier, I was in the heat. I was riding down Thunder Road. I looked at the rice paddies where young men had died. I looked at bomb craters that demolished a beautiful country. The lush tropical jungles had elephant grass and tall trees, but we withered them away with the chemicals we dropped to keep mosquitoes at bay. In the blink of an eye, I was back in a different world. I was in a world I missed. I had dreamt about this world while I lived in Nam. The Lord was with me, and I was so thankful I had made it home. The wounds I had were bad, but they would heal over time. My emotional wounds that I couldn't see or feel would take a lifetime to understand.

SOMETHING HAPPENED

After landing at Oakland International Airport, we had to go to a processing center, and I received my plane ticket to New York. After all the soldiers were processed, we returned to the airport. I had my ticket to board a commercial airline. It would stop in Chicago before reaching its final destination at JFK International Airport in Queens, New York. I can't remember exactly how I got from the airport to the Port Authority in New York City. I recalled four other soldiers from the 200 plus that landed in Oakland being with me when I arrived at Kennedy Airport. My remaining companions took a bus to parts of New Jersey and upstate New York when we reached the Port Authority. I walked to the subway along Eighth Avenue.

It was a fantastic walk through the hustle and bustle of the city. It was the fall, and it was a mild day. I took notice of the fashions of the guys and gals— miniskirts and colorful outfits. My eyes darted from person to person. As I walked down the street, I noticed the colorful artwork on the side of the buildings. It was a kaleidoscope of people and colors. Yet I felt that no one noticed me. I knew this is New York City, and I didn't expect New Yorkers to stop me and shake my hand. But then again, I'm in uniform and carrying a duffel bag, but I guess people see a lot of scenes in the city, and nothing surprises them.

Then I went into the subway on 8th Ave. I took the A train and changed trains at Yankee Stadium at 161st Street and River. I walked upstairs to get the Lexington Ave. Express on the elevated platform. Although it had been years, I remembered every detail of how to travel in the New York subway system. When I reached the elevated platform, I could see into the stadium. I had experienced this scene many times, and it was beautiful. The white chalk of the foul lines surrounded the brilliant colors of the seats.

I had stood on this platform many times. If I left the game early, my friends and I would watch the game while waiting for our train to pull into the station. You could hear the crowd's roar if someone made a great play or got a hit. I was back in a happy place. Two days before, I was in Vietnam.

I rode the train to East 183rd Street. Then, I took a familiar 20-minute walk back to my neighborhood. During my travels from the Port Authority to

Belmont Ave, Vietnam had faded from my mind. I reached my home, and the mailman had delivered the mail. He saw me and welcomed me home with a big bear hug. The mailman, Phil, delivered the same route for at least ten years. When I was a kid, Phil would drop his mail satchel and play catch with the kids. During the hot summer months, we would bring him some Kool-Aid. These were great memories. I didn't want to stay and talk to Phil for too long, and he told me to hurry up and ring the doorbell to surprise my mother.

I rang the doorbell, and my mom opened the door. She was surprised, to say the least. No one knew I was coming home that day. My family knew that I had been wounded but didn't have a lot of details. My mom hugged me, and at the same time, she looked at me from head to toe. I thought she was looking for signs of my injuries amidst her happiness to see me. I guess that's what mothers do! She asked me how I was and escorted me to the kitchen table. Immediately, the refrigerator offered a bowl of meatballs and sausage in gravy. Mom gave me a large slice of Italian bread, and she said, "Eat!" While I was savoring my mom's cooking, she called my dad and my sisters at their workplace.

After inhaling the meatballs and sausage, I went to my room, and my bed looked just like I had left it two years ago. I had imagined my room as I had left it many times while in Vietnam, and I changed out of my uniform into a pair of jeans and a favorite shirt. Then I told my mom I wanted to go to Arthur Ave. to see who was on the avenue.

Some transitions have occurred since 1964, when I graduated from high school. Bell bottoms and sandals were the new look. I liked the new look, and while in Vietnam, we would get magazines and see some of these fashions. Automakers developed new sports cars with new looks. The Camaros, Mustangs, and GTOs were among them. Those big-finned cars with bench seats gave way to cars with a more powerful engine.

The look of the doo-wop era was changing. Although these things changed, I liked what I saw and wanted to jump into the new scene. I still had a few months left in the military. Even with my GI haircut, I felt I could fit into the contemporary scene. I walked down to the bar, but no one was sitting outside. I passed the jewelry shop, but Sal wasn't there, and the shop was closed. I looked for my friend Johnny, and I went inside the bar. Patty was still tending the bar and told me that Johhny had to go to court. He got pinched with stolen merchandise. Patty told me that Vinny, Paulie, and Ally had been drafted into the military.

I inquired about Sal's shop and why it was closed. Patty told me that Sal had the big C (cancer). Sal was going through chemotherapy and was too sick to work full-time. Sal would go to work sporadically. His wife kept the business going, although the store hours were reduced.

I realized a lot had changed while I was away. As great as my subway ride and walk home were, I didn't know how I would handle the changes. I had 14 days of leave, and by the end of September, I would be headed to Ft. Bragg, North Carolina, to finish my army career. My feelings and emotions were back on a roller coaster of uncertainty. While in the jungle for two years, something happened in my neighborhood and the world. This transition would not be as easy as I had expected. I did not want to face the facts of my situation about Christina. I didn't dare ask anyone to update me on her whereabouts.

I took a walk past her house. I didn't know what I would say if I saw her. I didn't even understand why I would walk past her house. Maybe her parents or sisters would see me and tell Chris. But as I walked on her block, one of her neighbors recognized me. Millie was the watchdog of the block, and she knew what was happening in the neighborhood. She knew I had been in Vietnam. Millie welcomed me with open arms, which was a great feeling. She said I would have to look in Westchester to see Chris. Chris had moved, and her family had sold the house. The family had moved to upstate New York. Millie said that the old neighborhood was changing, and things were different.

I realized that everything had changed in two years. Something had happened, and change was now the ordinary course for me. The army had taught me about changes. The only problem with the changes I saw was that they brought a feeling of loss. That loss encompassed the years from 1964 through my return to the USA. It was the last quarter of 1967, and music, fashion, and attitudes radically changed. I had anticipated everything I experienced after high school would be the same.

I was home but felt I had only one foot in the door because my army orders destined me to Fort Bragg. I wanted to embrace the new world, but my other foot was still with the army. My mind felt the same conflict. I had great memories of civilian life, but I also thought of walking the jungles and flying on a Huey. My time on leave was moving quickly, and four days passed by too fast. It took me almost a week to begin to get reacclimated to city living as a civilian. Yet, I knew this was temporary, and I dreaded going to Fort Bragg. I would be in the South again. I remembered how strange the South had felt when I trained at Fort Benning, Georgia. I didn't want to make friends for the four months remaining in the army. I wondered why I needed to complete four more months. I felt I had done more than my share. I saw protests about the war, and I heard people call my military brothers baby killers. Something was happening in the US that I never expected while I sat in my door gunner seat half a world away in Vietnam.

FORT BRAGG

My leave flew by, and I finally saw Johnny and asked him about going to court. He told me he had been arrested with some guys trying to rip off a designer clothing warehouse. Johnny's dad was the bookie and loan shark who hung out at the bar. He was part of a crew of one of the five families. Johnny was in trouble because he associated with hoodlums who were overstepping their boundaries. A gang from Hunts Point decided to rob a warehouse that wasn't in their territory. His father, Big John, had to call in a favor; otherwise, Johnny would get a beating.

I realized that Johnny was involved with new guys, not from the neighborhood. His new friends were into dealing heroin and also using it themselves. His new friends came from an area in the south Bronx near the Hunts Point Terminal Market. That neighborhood was a rough place with drugs and prostitution. The community was Puerto Rican, with black and Dominican cultures. The neighborhood was a place with different music, cultures, and attitudes. It was a tough neighborhood, and I didn't understand why Johnny went there away from his Italian neighborhood.

The old-timers in the neighborhood kept complaining that things were changing, but I didn't understand. I asked my older sister what was changing in the neighborhood. She said that drugs had become openly used on the streets. Families that could afford to move had started to leave. Gang wars over turf had become violent, and guns and knives had replaced a fist fight. My sister told me she would see people on the street stoned on heroin. The Bronx was burning because landlords had lost rent, and they set their buildings on fire to collect insurance money.

While on leave, I had been searching for that time during 1964, after I graduated from high school. I didn't find it, and my old neighborhood looked different. I took the train into Brooklyn, as I had when I was dating Rosalie. I went back to the last stop on Lexington Ave. Express. Flatbush and Nostrand Avenues were called the Junction. That was a busy place, and it was a block from Brooklyn College. There were plenty of places to hang out or patronize. I could always see someone I knew. The junction was the unofficial meeting place for kids to gather during the evening. I could meet friends and go to a party, visit Greenwich Village, or see a live band. I was disappointed when

I returned to the junction. Everything looked the same, but the faces were unfamiliar.

I went into the Burger Flame, one of those meeting places. Eddie was still serving burgers and pizza. I asked him about some of the guys that hung around the Flame. Eddie told me that they went into the military or went to college. They stopped hanging around the junction.

So, my time on leave from the army wasn't as fulfilling as I had anticipated when I left Nam. I had to go back to Fort Bragg in a day, but I knew what to expect from the army. On the one hand, I was glad to be out of the war and happy to be home. At the same time, there was some comfort in returning to the army. After all, that's all I've known for the last 30 months.

I got a ride from my sister to LaGuardia Airport and boarded a plane to Raleigh, North Carolina. From there, I took a shuttle bus to the Greyhound Station. Then, I boarded a bus that took me to Fort Bragg. I reported to the 82nd Airborne Brigade training center. I was assigned to Company A and told to report for early formation at 5 a.m. I shared a room with another E-5 specialist on the second floor of the barracks.

My roommate was Willie Fernandez, and he was from the Bronx. Willie was Puerto Rican and had lived in the Pellam Park section of the Bronx. He had served in Vietnam, and he joined the army just before Christmas 1964. He had gone to basic training at Ft. Benning and volunteered for Airborne. Willie had seen action as I did in Corps III. He escaped the Nam without a scratch, but we never talked about the details of combat. We talked about smoking weed, getting high, and looking to party with girls. Willie told me he had been in this company since returning from Vietnam.

Most of the guys in my new company had been in Vietnam. The mission of this company was to support the training operation for the new recruits. Willie told me to ask the platoon sergeant to send me to vehicle training. I would be qualified to drive vehicles up to 5 tons. He said that driving was a great gig. My job would be to move the recruits to a location and pick them up hours later. There would be a lot of free time. Sometimes, we might pick up supplies or make deliveries to the mess halls.

Willie said that all the free time was an opportunity to party. He had a trailer with another soldier off base that was his drug stash. His buddy was being discharged from the army. Willie would lose a roommate and someone who helped pay the rent. Willie had met some local girls, and they would come over in the evenings. Willie asked me if I wanted to pay half the rent. I agreed and would head for the trailer anytime I wasn't working or had downtime. It was better than living in the barracks. On one of my first nights at the trailer, I met Georgia and Kathleen. Willie was trying to make it with either girl. So far, he was putting in his time and hoping to get a signal that one of the girls would sleep with him. Both girls were about 20 years old, but I wasn't sure and didn't care. Georgia had dark hair, and Kathleen was blond. Willie had a thing for blonds because all the Puerto Rican girls in his neighborhood had dark hair. The girls did a lot of teasing, and we knew it was the ladies' choice when or if we would get lucky.

It turned out that Georgia had moved from Jersey about two years earlier. Her father worked for the government and was reassigned to Ft. Bragg. Kath was on vacation and was spending two weeks with George. Willie's patience paid off, and with a couple of days left on her break, Kath let her hair down and decided to sleep with Willie. Kath returned with her secret memory of hooking up with Don Juan, Willie. Georgia began coming to the trailer more often after her friend went home. We started a romance, maybe out of loneliness or just convenience.

Willie connected with another soldier on base who dealt heroin and weed. One night, he asked Georgia and me if we wanted to try some heroin. Willie cut a straw and laid a few lines on the kitchen table. He told us we only needed a few lines and would feel great. He was right; the feeling was like having a drink and taking one of the pills that Gina had given me. George said she had tried it at a party when she lived in Jersey. Georgia and her girlfriends liked the high, and it made them horny. She had not had any H since coming to North Carolina.

I didn't realize it, but besides weed, heroin was in great demand. LSD (acid) had also become popular, but LSD and heroin produced opposite reactions. It became almost a nightly occurrence to snort some dope and to get in the sack with Georgia. The habit became so easy that Willie and I would get high during work. We would also get high on mornings when we had completed an assignment. We were in our room in the barracks, and Willie took out a syringe and injected heroin. "Shoot up" was the term used, or "get off" was another way of saying you would get high. I watched but didn't want to do this while in the barracks. I also noticed that I wasn't getting the same intensity as I had experienced when snorting. Willie told me I could use half the amount of heroin if I shot up. So, what the hell? I decided that I might try shooting up. I would need help and wanted to try it at the trailer while away from the army.

I probably got off a few weeks after taking my first snort. Willie showed me how to cook the heroin. It was a ritual, and Willie would lay out all the tools of the trade to shoot up. Hypodermic needles were hard to buy, so it was more practical to get an eyedropper. A bottle cap would hold the heroin, and Willie would sprinkle a few drops of water to dilute the drug. The next step was to cook it, and a match or a lighter would heat the bottle cap. It took a second or two, and Willie would drop a tiny piece of cotton into the bottle cap. I learned that the cotton would stop unwanted particles from entering the syringe. Willie would insert the eyedropper into the cotton and absorb the heroin. The last step was to tie off, using a belt or cord to squeeze the bicep. Anyone who has had blood drawn knows the process. My vein popped up, and Willie injected me. He slowly squeezed the nipple of the eyedropper, and he let the blood flow back into the dropper. By the time the heroin was going back into my arm, I felt warmth spreading through my body. I had never felt anything like it.

The closest thing to it was getting a shot of morphine when I was wounded. But this rush was immediate and very pleasurable. Georgia didn't want to shoot up, but Willie convinced her to try skin popping. Instead of finding a vein, he would inject it into the skin. He told her the best place to inject was her butt cheek. That night, Georgia and I would be on a course with very high roads of euphoria and depths in the valley of despair. At the time, I was having a good time. I didn't think about the Nam or my good old days with RoRo or Christina. Getting high would mask all the pain and disappointment of the past. I had a partner with Georgia, and we isolated ourselves from the world.

This routine of getting high went on for a while. It was before Thanksgiving, and Willie had about a month left in the army. His mom was going to Florida, and the house in the Bronx would be free to enjoy for a weekend. Willie had Georgia call Kath in New Jersey and ask if she would like to spend the weekend at his mom's house. Georgia and Kath talked almost daily. Kath used her company phone to make long-distance calls. Kath agreed, and it would be a good reunion with Georgia. And I'm sure she also had plans to be with Willie.

Willie had a used 1964 Chevy, and we traveled back to the Bronx. It was a long trip, and we had to pick up Kath in northern New Jersey. Maybe it was Hackensack or Garfield, New Jersey. I had no idea of anything in New Jersey, but it was a short drive over the George Washington Bridge and to Willie's house. It was about a ten-hour trip from Ft. Bragg, and we smoked a couple of joints. We had no heroin, which was good while Willie was driving.

We arrived at Willie's house at about midnight. We were too tired to do anything, so we smoked some hashish Kath brought and then slept. We went to a diner for a late breakfast the next day. We decided to go to a club in Yonkers that evening. We had a great time dancing and listening to a band. Kath had brought some quaaludes, and we got a good buzz. By midnight, we wanted to return to the house, and we had sex on our minds. Kath decided she needed another lude. She and Willie departed for his bedroom. Georgia and I slept in the living room.We were all groggy the following day, but Kath seemed to have had a rough night. She wanted to get home before her parents returned from vacation, so we dropped her off at her house before noon. But we still had about a ten hour drive back to Ft. Bragg.

We returned to the base before midnight and took Georgia to her house. Willie and I were exhausted from late evenings and partying, so we decided to sleep in the barracks. The following day, it was back to army life. Willie had about three weeks left to serve, and I would be out of the army about a month later.

After my return from Vietnam, my whole world revolved around drugs, especially heroin. My companion was Georgia. I had gotten very bold and had taken chances using drugs. I didn't realize it then, but my heroin use had caused me to withdraw from society. By the first week of December, I had learned how to shoot up myself, and I even shot up in my room in the barracks.

I also felt the effects of getting high for a week, and then I experienced the pangs of being without heroin. I wouldn't say it was a severe reaction, like the withdrawal depicted in the movies. I felt clammy and had a knot in my gut. I learned this reaction was called a "chippie." It wasn't painful but noticeable.

Willie was separated from the army a few days before Christmas. I did some soul-searching and stopped using heroin after he left. It was now Georgia that gave me comfort. I began to think about going home to the Bronx. How would I break up with her, and what did I have to look forward to back home? That was a stressful time, and I had no answers for my thoughts. Deep in my heart, I wanted to start over as I did after graduating high school. I wanted to get that good job to let me travel and share that with some ladies from outside my neighborhood. But I was also very anxious and couldn't get Christina out of my mind. I also thought about Rosalie, and at the same time, I thought, what about Georgia?

After Willie left, I had no transportation and decided to make myself feel good. So, I bought a 1966 Mustang that had been used as a demonstration model at the car dealership. The 1967 model had been out for some time, so I got a good deal on the Mustang. Besides, I had plenty of money saved from being in Vietnam. The purchase made me feel good. I would have transportation for my last month in North Carolina, and the Mustang would take me home to the Bronx. Georgia and I took many rides in the North Carolina countryside. My head was beginning to clear from all the heroin and downers. But I still had no answers about what to do about Georgia.

My last two weeks in the army were filled with anxious anticipation of returning to the Bronx. I reasoned that Georgia would stay with her parents unless I committed to take her north, I would be free, and I felt that Georgia had filled a void. Now I would have to move on. Although that idea sounded good, I felt guilty for some reason. The last time I saw her, I talked about getting settled with a job in the Bronx. I told her I would call and let her know when I got my place. But these were empty words and disingenuous babble. It left a slim hope that we might be together. I thought, at best, she could come for a long weekend. At least I knew that I would have sex. Then the day arrived. No more army, and I was on I-95 heading for the Bronx.

HOME IN THE BRONX

It was now January 27, 1968, and I was home in the Bronx. I had waited for this day to arrive for many months. I completed my military commitment at Fort Bragg and was heading home. I had no clue what to do, and I wanted to get a job. At the same time, I wanted to go to the bar on Arthur Ave. and meet some old friends. I knew that I would hear all the gossip from the wise guys. I wanted to return to a time when I had Christina and a great job at Eastern Airlines. I had resolved that Christina and I would never be together and that losing her was no longer eating up my heart. I thought about Rosalie, but so many years had passed since we were a couple, so I didn't want to add to the litter that cluttered my mind. I thought about calling Rosalie and hoped to take a ride to Brooklyn and see some familiar faces. I also wanted to go to clubs in the city and walk around Greenwich Village.

There were many options when I graduated high school, but those options were cut short when I entered the army. I felt like my life was starting over in a world that had radically changed since January 1965. I wanted to forget about Vietnam. I tried to move on with my life, but the memories didn't take long for Vietnam to haunt me.

The NVA and Viet Cong waged a major offensive throughout South Vietnam at the end of January 1968. They attacked our major military sites in South Vietnam. They attacked fire support bases and base camps. There was to be a cease-fire while the Vietnamese celebrated their Lunar New Year. I think someone forgot to tell the enemy. The TET offensive created some of the bloodiest fighting in every zone of South Vietnam. I couldn't escape the memories of the war. The news was plastered on TV every night. I could not escape from the 6 pm news that showed actual film footage of the fighting. Protests at home completed the picture, and street brawls between war supporters and pacifists began to divide the country.

The Tet Offensive lasted several months, and the 6 PM news offered the latest action each night around dinner time. Of course, the military and the media always gave the public that the upper hand of a battle went to the US troops. The body count became the official scorecard of the war. For every US soldier killed by the enemy, there were 3 or 4 times more dead enemies. I wanted to ignore the news, but my heart ached for all the boys who humped the boonies. The ambushes and booby traps and the darkness at night haunted me. I had to leave a light on at night when I went to bed.

I thought about Smitty and all the Huey crews, who were probably making three or four runs a day into the hostile fire. I could still hear the whoop-whoop sound of the rotor blades in my mind, and the sounds inside my flight helmet crackled in my ears. I remembered the chief and the metallic sound of spent casing that flew out of his M60. The cold metal sound of water cans and ammo cans dropping to the floor of my Huey never left my mind. I could not wash away those sounds as quickly as Charlie Kenny and I washed away the blood stains on the floor of our Huey.

I felt paralyzed, unable to move forward with my life. I always thought I would return to work at Eastern Airlines. Now, I didn't want to drive to Queens or be around planes. In my mind, I could still hear the Hueys starting their engines on the flight line. The memory of the whining sound of the engines starting gave me goosebumps. As I write about this memory, I am getting goosebumps. I tried to get away from those sounds that reminded me of Vietnam. At the same time, living in the Bronx reminded me of all the great times I had growing up in the neighborhood before my military service. The memory of Christina and other girls I had dated lingered. My friends from high school had moved away or had other interests. I was past the days at the PAL or listening to Doo Wop in the stairways at a school dance.

I felt like that proverbial dog that had never ventured out of his yard. Then, one day, the gate was left open, and the dog ran out. The dog runs up and down the block and runs into the street and the dangerous traffic. It doesn't appear that the dog knows where he or she is going, but they are going somewhere. That's how I felt. I realized that I had to move forward, but I also needed something that had previously made me feel secure. Two things had given me comfort, but Georgia was in North Carolina, and the euphoric feeling of shooting dope had been absent for some time.

I needed a job to move out of my Bronx neighborhood since I couldn't live at home with my parents. Being alone and away from home for three years demanded I move out. I decided to go to Manhattan and go to a personnel agency in the hope I could get me a job.

I lucked out, and in my first interview, I was sent to a shop in the garment district. The owners were interested in hiring veterans. I was nervous at the interview, but they liked that I could drive large vehicles. I got hired on the spot and began to learn about the garment industry. I always took it for granted when I wore new pants and shirts, and I never considered how these goods were produced. I learned about materials, and I watched the process of making pants and jackets. I was amazed that someone could make a suit from a bolt of fabric. The process was fascinating to observe, and most of the cutters and the ladies at the sewing machine were immigrants who spoke broken English. I learned how clothing was made while I waited for New York State to approve my CDL (commercial driving)license. The company that I worked for was a family-owned business. As an immigrant from Armenia, Johnny learned his trade from his dad. Johnny had worked in the factory as a child when he wasn't in school. He was proud of his heritage and taught me much about the business. It was customary to work an eleven-hour day, six days a week. I wasn't opposed to work, but I also wanted to play. I had missed out on a lot of partying. While I was in Vietnam, the world had changed, and I felt I had to catch up.

I also felt that living at a high pace and working hard would help me forget about the war. The custom tailoring company Petrosyan and Son had several contracts. The company made dress uniforms for the Navy Department, and I would make the delivery in a 5-ton truck. I drove to Bush Terminal in Brooklyn every two weeks and delivered uniforms to a Navy outlet store.

On my first trip to Bush Terminal, I pulled up at the loading dock, and to my surprise, I knew the guy standing on the dock. It was a friend I had met when I worked on Wall Street. Louie D lived in Brooklyn and was part of a crew of kids who all hung out at the Junction. I met Louie through Rosalie when I went out with many kids from the East Flatbush neighborhoods.

Louie told me that he, Bobby, and Charlie still got together. He told me that some girls from the crowd had gotten engaged to their boyfriends. I asked about Ro, and Louie told me that after our breakup, she started hanging out with a new crowd and dated Ralph. I met most of those kids, and I knew Ralphie. Everyone knew each other, and there were always new introductions to the group. Some guys had gotten into college, and some were disqualified for physical reasons. A few were lucky not to get drafted. RoRo had a baby with Ralph, and they were living together, so I didn't pursue the conversation about her. I was glad that this chance meeting with Louie would reconnect me with friends I had met while dating RoRo. I began to spend more time with my Brooklyn friends than with the guys from the old neighborhood in the Bronx.

After two months of work at my new job, I was ready to get my place. I wanted to be close to work in midtown Manhattan and closer to my old friends in Brooklyn. I decided that Manhattan was too expensive and didn't want a roommate to help with the rent. My friend Charlie had a girlfriend who lived near Prospect Park in Brooklyn. He told me an apartment was for rent in one of the brownstone houses on her block. It was perfect because it was a few blocks from the subway and wasn't far from Flatbush and Nostrand Avenues. It was congested, and parking wasn't easy, but the price was right. It was also a neighborhood in transition and made up of blacks, Puerto Ricans, and whites.

I had a new apartment in Brooklyn, and I had connected with some old friends from East Flatbush. I began to hang out and get high again. I wanted to meet Rosalie again, but I knew she had a baby and thought she was living with her boyfriend. But, I quickly learned that her boyfriend disappeared after her baby was born. I felt terrible about this, and Charlie told me where she lived. It took a couple of weeks to muster up the nerve, but I finally went to see her. Ro lived in a basement apartment on Beverly Road, close to Flatbush Avenue. Ro had written letters to me when I entered the army and arrived in Vietnam. We always remained friends, even when I dated Christina. I felt I needed to give her support as a single mom.

I went to her apartment after work one evening. She lived in a basement apartment in a two-family house. It wasn't far from my apartment, and I had heard that her girlfriend was her roommate and helped watch the baby when Ro went to work. RoRo didn't know I was coming, and I hoped she would be home. I rang the doorbell, and the door opened with Ro standing before me. Her contagious smile and demonstrative nature had not changed and, Ro began laughing. She waved her arms and almost tackled me in the doorway. She was a tough girl and a survivor. RoRo took me by my arm and hustled me inside. I knew her friend Linda because she grew up on the same block as Ro. The three of us laughed and talked about the good old days when we would double date. We smoked a joint, and I felt like I had never left for a war. At least I felt like that for a few hours. My life has gone through many changes since returning to the US. Who would have thought I would move to Brooklyn? I never thought I would see RoRo again. I started feeling good about myself; my home was no longer the Bronx.

GEORGIA

By the middle of 1968, I had been out of the military for about six months, and a lot had occurred. I had a job in Manhattan, and I lived in Brooklyn. I was reunited with some old friends, but something was missing. I began dating again, but I didn't want an exclusive relationship. I imagined having a few girlfriends, some with benefits, and some just hanging out as buddies. Our group of friends provided that type of situation. During the week, we all worked and got together on the weekend to party. Maybe we would go to a concert or visit a club that had a band and a place to dance. At times, I would meet new people who were friends of friends. So, there was never a dull moment on the weekends.

Drugs were always part of the evening, whether on the weekend or weeknight. I hardly stayed home during the week. A couple of girls in the group had slept with a couple of my friends. That was one of those friend-with-benefit situations, but no one seemed to care. We were all just having a good time. Rosalie went out with the group a few times, but she had a baby to care for. She was crazy and carefree, but she was also studying to be a paralegal. We were good friends, but we never dated or had sex again. I would do anything for her, and she cared for me as much as possible while trying to be a single mom. We had an unspoken bond and would never be jealous if we dated someone else. She drifted away from the group and eventually began dating a guy at the law firm where she worked.

I was happy for Ro, but my routine had become stale, and drugs, especially heroin, reappeared. I occasionally dropped some acid, and we would go into Manhattan. Going into the city, with all its signs and colors, intensified our trip. We would drive over the Brooklyn or Manhattan Bridges. I don't know how we did that, and God must have had his hand on the steering wheel. Greenwich Village was always safe because it was a place of no judgment. The Electric Circus on St. Marks off Second Avenue was the perfect place to intensify my acid trip. Although this was fun and sex was easy to find, I felt something was missing. In hindsight, I didn't know what I wanted. My friends and I insulated ourselves by partying. When I say "partying," it means to go out and enjoy yourself, and drugs, alcohol, and sex are the end game. Guys would always use this reference to describe a girl who liked to enjoy herself.

"She likes to party" was a signal that if you hung around with her, you could wind up having sex.

Living this lifestyle was fun, but the uncertainty of what would happen each time I went out created some anxiety. After ten months of being a free bird, Thanksgiving and Christmas were upon me. The holidays reminded me of the sweet relationships I had lost with RoRo and Christina. I stayed in touch with Georgia and spoke to her briefly over the phone. We talked about all the times we spent together in North Carolina. I called her to wish her a happy Thanksgiving, and she told me she would spend it with her family. She said she had not been out for a long time since I left her. She was focused on getting her two-year degree at college. She told me she had met some guys over the summer, which lasted about two months. She didn't get into details, but it seemed she was hurting. Georgia finished school before Christmas. She had no plans other than to spend time at home and look for a job in the New Year.

I asked her if she would consider moving to New York or New Jersey. She had previously lived in Jersey, and her friend Kath worked there. I told her I had an apartment in Brooklyn and had reunited with old friends with whom I always had a good time. I told her getting a job in the metropolitan area might be easier than in North Carolina. Georgia said she didn't want to stay in Fayetteville. Her best option would be to look for a job in Raliegh, meaning she would need to get an apartment. She also told me that she had no friends. I didn't invite her to stay with me, but I gave her my new phone number.

It didn't take long, and Georgia called me a couple of days before Christmas. She told me that she had talked it over with her parents and that she would be moving to New Jersey. She had gotten in touch with Kath, and they would be roommates. Kath's boyfriend had purchased a brownstone as an investment in downtown Jersey City. Kath lived in one of the apartments and had been working for a brokerage house in Jersey City. Kath told Georgia that she knew a lot of people and hoped her connections could help Georgia get a job. I thought this was great news, and it was a quick drive or subway ride for me to see her in New Jersey.

Georgia moved to Jersey City during the first week of January, and I went to see her. It was a quick ride through the Holland Tunnel, and in less than ten minutes after getting on the other side of the Hudson River, I was at the apartment. It was great seeing Georgia and Kath, and I invited Kath to ride into Brooklyn, but Kath didn't want to be the third wheel. I wanted to show Georgia what a great place Brooklyn was and maybe go and meet some of my friends. I felt like a cab driver giving her the grand tour, but I didn't mind. We arrived at a pub near the Junction and across the street from Brooklyn College. There was a band, and I ran into some friends. It was a great evening.

I applied with the phone company in Brooklyn for a position as a repairman in early December. The job had better benefits and pay than working in the garment industry. The phone company offered me a job in downtown Brooklyn. I would work in a repair office. I told Georgia other jobs were available at the phone company. If she got a job in Brooklyn, the commute from Jersey City to get to work would take less than forty minutes. She took my advice and interviewed for several positions. About three weeks later, she accepted a job as a business representative. Georgia would be in downtown Brooklyn on Willoughby Street, and I worked in a repair office about fifteen minutes away.

I loved my repair job because each call was different. I wasn't cooped up in an office and working 10 hours daily, and if I worked more than eight hours, I got paid overtime. Georgia and I started to see each other every weekend. She would pack her overnight bag on a Friday, and I picked her up after work. Then, we would spend the weekends together at my apartment. We got along excellently, and I didn't need that urge to party with anyone else.

GROWING UP

Georgia and I found comfort in each other, and by the end of 1969, we were in our mid-twenties, and we were together each weekend. We partied hard and had lots of friends. She met many of my friends from Brooklyn, and I took her to the Bronx and the bar on Arthur Avenue. I even took her to my parents' house. We traveled and went on vacation together. I learned a lot about her through Kath and their friends. When I met her in North Carolina, I didn't realize that she partied as I did when she was nineteen and twenty years old. When I met her, I knew she had a few romances, and maybe they ended badly, or she was just having a good time with some benefits. We lived for the weekends, and I thought I found that perfect lifestyle.

The history lessons I had learned from the army and Vietnam always influenced my trust in people. I saw how things could change or disappear. I knew my day could start positively, but that good feeling could blow up by the afternoon. Similarly, my relationships with Ro and Chris also lasted over a few months, but they had dissolved. It reminded me that what seems perfect may disappear in the blink of an eye. I was happy with the relationship with Georgia, and I knew she could decide to return to her younger days of exploration. That did not bother me because I knew I wouldn't cry or be heartbroken. I would explore and find someone else. Yet things were good, and we both seemed content in our situation.

Although we were now young adults, and I use that term loosely, drugs were a big part of the relationship. Drugs, sex, and rock and roll never left our scene. Many of my friends were still using heroin. At times, Georgia and I found ourselves using it again. She was not into shooting up but liked the feeling. She and Kath always wanted quaaludes. It was almost a ritual. If they ate some quaaludes, they were primed for sex. I didn't care for ludes, but if it floated their boat, I didn't care. What guy would turn their back on a good time?

I can't remember the month. Maybe it was at the beginning of 1971. Kath invited us to attend a weekend up in the Catskill Mountains at a resort. Kath had been on these weekend trips with her boyfriend, Jeff, and people from his company. We would board a bus in Jersey City with young people from Jeff's job, and most would be partying couples or hookups. Of course, we had pot, and the girls came loaded with quaaludes. It was cold upstate. Snow was on the ground, and we frolicked in it. The main house had games and activities, complete with a prominent fireplace. Before midnight, most had retreated to their rooms to enjoy each other's company.

Georgia and I had a great time and had a bottle of wine in our room. We had some weed, and she popped another lude. We fell asleep from exhaustion and the influence of wine and drugs. It was the last night, and the bus would leave before noon and return to Jersey City. My early military training and always working had me up before seven o'clock, and I wanted some breakfast. Georgia had difficulty waking up. She almost fell trying to get out of bed since she was still groggy from the previous night. She was slurring, and her eyes rolled back in her head as she fell on the bed. I had to get her to the sink and throw water on her face, but Georgia was dead weight. Usually, I could pick her up and move around, but she would help by wrapping her arms around me. I had no luck trying that, and I had to call Kath in the adjoining room. Jeff and Kath came into the room, and we decided she needed to get in the shower. So, Jeff and I picked her up and struggled to get her in the bathtub. Complete with a tee shirt and panties we worked to get a half-conscious 115-pound girl into the tub.

I got in the tub so she wouldn't crack her head on the tile. Jeff turned on the faucets, and it seemed to startle her. We talked to her, and she babbled until she realized she was in the bathtub. She was able to stand up while we helped her. Kath took off her soaked tee shirt and wrapped a towel around her. We put a second and third towel around her and dried her hair. We placed her on the bed, and Kath got her undergarments back on, but I needed help to get her jeans and boots on. Jeff went and got some coffee for all of us. She was awake but still sloppy in her speech. We got her on the bus and sat in the back, and she slept with her head on my shoulder for most of the ride.

It troubled me that Georgia depended on her quaaludes to make her feel relaxed. I began to see a different side of her. It was evident that Kath and Georgia did lots of partying, but that stuff in the past didn't bother me. We all have baggage, and I wanted to be supportive because she had given me some stability. After the Catskill trip, I talked to her about us cooling off with the hard drugs the following weekend. Smoking a joint was okay, and an occasional lude was OK, but nothing more.

I also thought that Georgia would return to having a wandering eye if she stayed with Kath. Georgia accused me of having a girl stay over in my apartment. I told her I was happy with our relationship, and I said if I felt the need to be with someone else, she would be the first to know. I asked her if she was waiting for us to get married, and she said she wasn't in a hurry. I was okay with that answer.

I wanted to be with a woman and explore and grow together. We could live together or have our own space. I wasn't too sure about marriage, either. I didn't want my life to resemble the lifestyle of my parents. Kids could be okay, but that was a big responsibility, and I could barely take care of myself. I always thought we couldn't let having a child extinguish our passion for each other. In my mind, I reasoned that I was taking a practical and adult view of how life should be. The free-bird spirit was instilled in me by all the changes I had undergone. This happened in the army, in Vietnam, and from watching the people in my old neighborhood. Maybe I didn't communicate that clearly to Georgia, but I assumed she had the same mindset.

We always practiced safe sex, and Georgia was that calendar girl who counted out the days when she was less likely to get pregnant. I had been in the habit of using a condom after getting over the embarrassment of my first purchases when I was 17. About a year after the Catskill trip, Georgia moved in with me in the spring of 1972. We weren't getting married or ready to have kids. But, borrowing a line from Robert Burns, the best-laid plans of mice and men often go awry. Georgia got pregnant and had twin boys on December 1, 1973. We didn't plan on that, and we did the grown-up thing and got married in the summer of 1973.

TC

My boss at the phone company liked my enthusiasm at work and set me up as an acting foreman. He knew that I had twins and worked a lot of overtime to save money so I could buy a house. The office in East New York had a lot of repairs and installation work, but there was a high turnover rate, and absenteeism was a problem. There would be plenty of overtime if I wanted, or I could become a foreman and earn a better salary. We needed a house because we had twins in a four-room walk-up apartment. I worked plenty of overtime and eventually became a foreman.

Georgia stayed at home with the babies, so we had only one income. I got a VA loan approved rather quickly due to my service-connected injuries from Vietnam. We began looking for a house that would have me closer to the East New York office. We looked around Marine Park, an area in demand and a great neighborhood to raise children. It was slightly over our price range, so we looked further in the Canarsie area.

I looked at some homes around Ave. N and East 57th Street. It was a great neighborhood, predominantly Italian. I was set to buy something nearby when my real estate guy told me about a two-family house on East 92nd Street. It was a little further from where I was looking, but the price was the same as the one-family home. The ability to collect rent and be closer to my job was appealing. A school was a block away, and it was a short ride to the subway or to get on the Belt Parkway. We jumped at the opportunity and bought a house. We moved into the new home late in 1975 and spent our first Christmas in our own home. I worked a lot of overtime and then got promoted in 1978.

My office did many residential repairs and installations, and as new industries emerged, the commercial side grew. I oversaw new retail services and moved to an office upstairs. I got off the work floor sometime in 1980. That's when I met Terri Capone. It was extremely rare for a woman to start working as an installer for New York Telephone. Terri was young and pretty, and she grew up in an Italian neighborhood in Bath Beach, Brooklyn. Terri didn't stay long as an installer and began working in the office when two female clerks quit. I met Terri because she was the logistics coordinator for all the new projects in the East New York area. I was the new guy on the block, and Terri helped get me familiar with the work to be done. She also told me who was good to work with and who not to trust.

Terri spoke her mind; some people were intimidated by her. I never felt that way about her. It took some time, but I learned about her background as time progressed. I knew she was married and lived in Hempstead County on Long Island. She had married young and had a son several years older than my twins. She had grown up as a tough Italian girl of first-generation Italians and, like me, had several sisters. I had grown up in the Bronx, and she had grown up in Brooklyn. But the culture and backdrop were the same. We were both fighters and spoke our minds. So, it was easy to relate to her. The neighborhood didn't offer many options for lunch, so either a lunch was delivered, or you packed a lunch. Sometimes, the job got so busy that there was no time for lunch.

I had to go into the field and meet with businesses opening a new office. Sometimes, a building was being renovated, and Terri and I made several trips together. A favorite place to have lunch was the Lindenwood Dinner near Howard Beach. We had a great working relationship and kept our relationship professional. We were friendly but seemed content with our private lives. Although I wish I had known her when I was single, I didn't get any signals that she liked me other than as a co-worker. She seemed comfortable with her husband and family.

I felt that Georgia and I had fallen into a rut, and our days of partying were well behind us. She had two kids and took care of the shopping, cooking, and cleaning. The boys were in school, and Georgia took them to school and picked them up after school. She was a great mom, but her attention to being a traditional housewife left little time for us. I would leave the house by seven in the morning and sometimes return until seven. I was promoted again and was in charge of the entire facility in East New York. There were more meetings, and I spent less time working with Terri. I was earning a good wage and saw myself caught up in a world with little time to play.

Whenever I got to work with Terri or go out to lunch with her, it was like a breath of fresh air. I felt alive being around her. She was fun to be with, and even though we were married, we had that feeling that we had to explore and do more. The ho-hum everyday family life was good, but a new challenge at work with Terri was always exciting. I never considered having an affair with Terri because I respected her. I liked her and would never want to complicate our lives. By now, I had been married for about eight years, and Terri had been married much longer, although she was a few years younger than me. She never spoke about her family life, so I couldn't tell if she was happy or restless.

It was right before Christmas of 1984 that Terri and I had an embrace and a kiss that were more than wishing someone a Merry Christmas. We had worked in the same office for a few years and had a great working and personal relationship. Terri confided in me that her husband had separated from her, but they had not divorced. Her husband had moved to live with a friend who lived in Sheepshead Bay. It was the holiday season, and I felt terrible that she would spend it alone, although her son would be home. I wasn't sure if she and her husband were attempting to get back together, and I didn't press the issue. I couldn't understand why anyone would want to leave such a bright, fun-loving person. She was attractive and could hold her own with guys who thought she might be easy. I watched her operate and put guys in their place. That Brooklyn girl reminded me of my younger days in the Bronx. I felt that we had similar traits and we could always communicate. We might have different opinions on some subjects or about how to do a job, but those differences were minimal, and we always understood each other.

The company was having a Christmas luncheon at an Italian restaurant on Cross Bay Blvd afterwork around 5pm. We could invite a spouse or friend. Terri would not have her husband there, and Georgia was home. If the mood struck, people could get up and dance. There was some dancing, mainly freestyle. We danced and had a great time. Then, a slower song, "Have Yourself a Merry Little Christmas," was next. We stayed on the dance floor. It became clear that there was some magic between us. I know some eyes were upon us, and I thought up to now, no one in the office thought anything of us. We acted in a way that wouldn't let anyone think that something was going on between us, and there wasn't.

As the party began to break up, I got our coats from the coat check. I helped Terri with her jacket and felt like I was on a date, trying to make a good impression. We walked to our cars and went to her car first. She opened her door and turned to me to say goodnight and thank me for a good time. But before she said more, I leaned into her, grabbed her arm, and kissed her. It wasn't a long, passionate kiss, but it was slow and more than a quick peck.

As I drove home, I thought about her and wanted to know her better, but I was married. The holidays went by, and I had some time off from work. Although this was a time to be with my family, I kept thinking of Terri. I returned to work after the New Year, and Terri told me her husband had come home to be with his son and her, and it seemed like they would reconcile. So, on the one hand, I was happy for her; on the other hand, I knew our relationship wouldn't go further than a kiss and a dance.

THE HEAT IS ON

I worked with Terri on a few projects with the holidays behind me. That unseen barrier that we had always honored seemed to have left us by now. We sat close to each other when we went to lunch or drove somewhere in the company car. The hugs and touching became frequent. I didn't know if she liked me or wanted excitement away from her marriage. My life got much more complicated when I attended a meeting in Garden City, Nassau County. Terri was at the meeting, and we sat next to each other. We exchanged non-verbal looks when some speaker was full of himself. We did have that great sense that we knew what each of us was thinking, but I wasn't sure how she felt about me.

After lunch, we sat in the hotel lobby before the next training session. Terri told me that she had filed for divorce. Her husband had been with another woman while living with his friend. She confronted him, and he was caught red-handed. She didn't get into details, except that he wanted the house. She had gone to a lawyer, and being the mom with a child would help her in the divorce. Besides, she told me she had made the down payment when she bought the house. She said she didn't want anything from her husband or child support. The divorce went uncontested.

The training session ended early, and she asked if I could stop by her house. She said she only lived a few minutes from Garden City. It didn't matter if she was an hour away. I said sure, and I followed her. We drove onto the Southern State Parkway and exited in an exit or two. I remember seeing a sign saying Baldwin, but I knew nothing about Nassau County. We drove a few minutes and went down a few blocks of oak trees that lined each side of the street. The homes were spread out, and we pulled into her driveway. It was a lovely home with a yard, and a lawn and shrubs separated each house. The driveway was a blacktop that fit two cars and had a garage.

As an 18-year-old who grew up in the brick-and-mortar neighborhood of the Bronx. This scene was one that I had always imagined. I would meet some good-looking girl who lived in the suburbs and had a big house with a yard and swimming pool. I didn't know if Terri had a swimming pool because we didn't go outside. We sat on the couch, and she put on the radio. We talked a bit, and we began to move close to one another, and we kissed. Before long, a trail of clothes had been discarded on the stairs leading up to her bedroom. My thoughts of uncertainty about her feelings toward me were no longer in doubt.

From that day forward, I led a double life for almost two years. I found myself making excuses why I had to work on a weekend or late into the night. Our assignments didn't always have us working together, and our projects often didn't cross paths. But we spoke almost daily and spent time together whenever possible. We did simple things like walking in the park or driving to Jones Beach or Rockaway. I went shopping with her, which I had never done before. I even took her to the doctor when she was ill.

It was an unbelievable feeling, and I thought about leaving my marriage. We were both well into upper management of the New York Telephone Company. We would go to a seminar or advanced management programs in another state, and we certainly took full advantage of the hotel's accommodations. Other managers from our district knew us but never knew about our relationship. I guess that all came to light when we both missed a morning class due to the night before. We went to shows together, went to Atlantic City, and stayed overnight. I had the nerve to tell Georgia that I had training. We worked hard, but we partied harder. Besides a few cocktails, drugs were not the catalysts for any pleasures. Our relationship didn't need substances or alcohol. We genuinely cared for each other, and drugs didn't need to fuel our passion.

I thought about my time with Rosalie and how that relationship started with getting high. Most encounters with the opposite sex usually started with drugs when I was growing up. It was accepted and became a way of life. Indeed, drugs clouded my mind. Christina was that exception, much like Terri. However, the army and Vietnam caused that relationship to have many interruptions. Eventually, Chris decided to move on, and I let her go. I didn't fight for her. Now, I had fallen in love. Drugs did not fuel my feelings. This relationship was honest and innocent. But, my family was an impediment and an irritating spec of dust that clouded my eye.

Our time seeing each other became more frequent, and I felt like I was living two lives. I had commitments at home but wanted Terri to be part of my life. I had to make a choice. My dilemma and lack of action to make a decision kept me in limbo. I stayed that way until the day that Terri transferred to another office further out on Long Island. At that same time, someone called my home and told Georgia I was having an affair. I never found out who called, and if Georgia knew, she wouldn't tell me. I suspected that it could have been someone at work. Terri decided to take another position in Hicksville, Long Island. She reasoned that I would be out of sight and out of mind. She said she understood my feelings and that I wouldn't leave my home. She said she never wanted to hurt me and wanted me to be happy.

I tried to accept her statements, but my heart was breaking, and I hated myself for causing her pain. I knew she was tough and would never let me see her cry, but I knew I had damaged her heart. I was so confused. Should I leave home? If I did, I would have nothing and would be paying through the nose for my kids and wife. I would need a place to live, and what if T (Terri), I would call her that sometimes, got tired of me? After all, this beautiful young lady could do anything and get restless, just like many women in my relationships. I thought she had every right to be with another guy because I went home at the end of the day. If I let her go, she would be in the arms of someone else, and I didn't want to entertain that idea. Uncertainty about what to do ripped at my heart, but I was sure I was in love.

Several weeks had passed, but I kept thinking of her. My home life had become cold, and I was going through the motions. Georgia and I never talked about what happened or why it happened. Although it seemed like she forgave me, she never forgot. I understood that, but I also reasoned that she needed me to stick around. In my mind, I knew our life would never be the same.

I thought about all the good times Terri and I enjoyed, and we always understand each other before we uttered a word. There was a certain magic about us. We felt it, and several people at work could feel our attraction. We didn't need to be demonstrative or say anything. So many people said how we looked at each other gave away our feelings. A co-worker, Marco, had asked if I had talked to Terri since she transferred. Marco and Terri had grown up in the same neighborhood in Brooklyn as kids, and by chance, they wound up working in East New York. Marco told me he had spoken to her since her move to Hicksville. He gave me the number and said he thought she wouldn't mind if I called her, so I did.

AT&T

Tand I kept in touch and tried to control our emotions. Although Terri was working in Hicksville, we met for dinner a few times. We didn't get a room or anything like that, and we just enjoyed each other's company. She was dating another guy and we resolved that we didn't want to restart our passion. Our situation would not change because I chose to remain at home. Still, we enjoyed being with each other, and our banter was always quick. We would still meet and take a walk in the park. The last time we were together was in the fall of 1987. We went to the movies that day; it would be the last time I saw her. The film was a love story between two characters who would never stay together. But, for one brief summer, they found the love of their life.

Although our love story went well beyond one summer, I thought the situation was similar. The difference was that we were married or had been married, and the characters in the movie were younger. Under our circumstances, we were unlikely to fall for each other. The characters in the fairytale movie were as improbable as our situation. Toward the film's end, the characters departed in one scene, and there was sadness. But there was one more reunion, and it was evident that a certain magic never left. I left the theater thinking these two characters were made for each other. They had a time in their life that they would never experience again. The movie had me rooting for them to get back together somehow. Everything that Terri and I had been through screamed that, just like the characters. We were made for those roles in the movie. We watched and held hands. At times, we looked at each other, and the unspoken glance said this could be us. After that day with Terri at the movies, we didn't speak for more than two months.

The holidays would be upon us, and I decided to call her to wish her a Merry Christmas. A guy answered her line at work and said she had left NY Telephone. I didn't get much information and didn't want to ask too many questions. My office had its traditional Christmas gathering, and I ran into my friend Marco. I wondered if he knew that Terri left the phone company. Maybe she had married, was dating, or moved away. Marco told me that Terri had broken up with her boyfriend. She had made many connections and was well respected for her work. She pursued an offer by AT&T to be a project manager in Maryland. Marco told me her son had graduated from high school and left home. There was no reason to continue working in an office with unpleasant memories. Marco gave me her number, but I didn't call her.

I tried to put her out of my mind, but that was impossible. For the next year, I put my efforts into my work and focused on my twin boys in high school. Time had passed, and Georgia and I seemed to have broken the icy relationship because of my mistakes. It wasn't back to how it was when we first got married, but the tension had subsided. From time to time, part of my heart remembered all the beautiful times I had with Terri. I wondered if she was dating, and that thought always stung my heart.

My life's journey has had many twists and turns. I never imagined I could experience so many traumatic events and relationships. I never thought my life could be so complicated. Things were changing at Ma Bell, and there were rumors of consolidations, buyouts, or forced retirements. I called Marco because he always seemed to have his ear to the ground about corporate plans. He told me that many top managers were looking to leave New York Telephone. AT&T was looking to poach top managers from NY Telephone. He inquired about opportunities and gave me a number in the city to ask about employment opportunities.

I contacted the human resources specialist at AT&T, who was interviewing for upper management positions. We discussed my background and what opportunities were available. I didn't want to move the family, and I took a job in Manhattan that involved overseeing overseas communications. The pay was a couple thousand dollars a year more than NY Telephone. I felt the position had the potential to grow, and the communication field was expanding outside the continental United States.

I accepted a position at AT&T in midtown Manhattan and began traveling on subways to my new job in 1989. Ironically, I had become an employee at AT&T, and Terri had left NY Telephone and took a position with AT&T in Maryland. About a year later, Marco told me he had spoken to Terri. Marco gave me her work telephone number. He said that they spoke when she first arrived in Maryland. AT&T put her up in a hotel for two months so she could shop around for an apartment. Marco said she became friendly with a woman living at the same hotel who had relocated from Virginia. Her friend was part American Indian, part African, and part Irish. From our conversation, it seemed her friend had lived in the Washington, DC, area and knew all the night spots. Terri loved the excitement, and they were inseparable. They had planned to share an apartment near Rockville, where AT&T was located. Her friend's brother had a big house in Chevy Chase, which was a lovely area. Her brother traveled a lot and had a top-level government job, and he wouldn't be home often. They could house-sit and save some cash so they moved in the brothers home. They could take the Metro, be at work in less than half an hour, and live a few minutes from Georgetown.

I was happy for her, but I didn't want to contact her because I thought I would open an old wound or, worse, that I wouldn't feel the same for her. I kept her work number in Rockville. I couldn't let it go. I had fooled myself about us not working out. Maybe that was thinking that camouflaged the pain in my heart. A few more years went by, and we never made contact. As time had dulled my thoughts of our time together, a piece of my heart held onto the precious memories.

It was in the late nineties, and the twins had finished college. One son was offered an excellent job on Wall Street at a brokerage house, and my other son would be enrolling in a graduate program at Georgetown Law School. My life had come a long way from running the streets of the Bronx as a 16-year-old wiseass. I had made it through two tours in Vietnam. I had some great relationships, but I always compared all my long and short relationships to Terri's. She was out of my life but always in my heart.

I was driving my son to Georgetown, and Georgia was staying home. She had recently recovered from ovarian cancer and was still recuperating. I wondered what became of Terri. Was she even in Maryland or still working for AT&T? She always seemed adventurous and ready to do anything. I thought about calling her, but I secretly hoped she had vanished so I could forget us. If she answered, what would I discover? Was she married, divorced, or just having a good time? What kind of guy would she be with? I know it was wild for me to think all these things, but I couldn't help myself. It had been a long time since we watched that movie in 1987, and I wrestled with whether to call her or get it out of my head.

GEORGETOWN

I dropped my son off at his Georgetown residence, and I went to check into my hotel. It was early afternoon, and I was finally settled into my room. I decided to call her work number. It was a long shot, but I had to do this or regret missing an opportunity to hear her again. I called, and a receptionist answered, and I told her I was looking to speak to Terri Capone. The lady said we know a Terri Capone Johnson. Would you like me to connect you? I replied, okay, that sounds like it could be her. The young lady said I sounded like her and that I must be from New York. I quickly said yes, and she asked who I should say is calling. I replied, tell her Mikey D.

When Terri said hello, her voice gave me that mental picture of us standing together. She said hello in an almost incredulous salutation. I said in an excited tone, "Hey T, how are you doing?" She said, "Mikey, how have you been? It's been a long time." I melted when she called me Mikey, and I replied, I know, and I see you have a new name. Terri said that's a long story. I answered that I had the time to listen. I said I was staying at Bethesda because I dropped my son off in Georgetown. I asked if she was able to grab a bite to eat and get a drink. I said we could plan for tomorrow after work because I had plans with my son for tonight.

Terri said she had bought a home just west of Bethesda and would work through lunch and leave early the next day. She gave me directions to her house, and I would pick her up at 1:30 p.m. I said this would be great. I said I didn't want to talk long and hold her up from work and that we would have tomorrow to catch up. While talking, I had a smile and a vision of my sweetheart. When I hung up, all my fears that we wouldn't have that old feeling instantly vanished. That felt like us, but it had been over ten years since we were together.

The next day, she called my room to tell me she was leaving work. She would be home in 20 minutes and change into something more comfortable. I was only a few minutes away and arrived at just about 1:30. I was impressed with her house and walked up and rang the doorbell. She opened the door,

her eyes sparked, and she had a big grin. I reached out, and she gave me both hands. I pulled her close, and then we hugged. We decided to drive to

Georgetown and park by the waterfront. We walked back to M Street where there were plenty of bars, restaurants, and shops to choose from. But just like in old times, the place didn't matter. It was our being together.

We found a place and had a couple of drinks and lunch. We talked and reminisced about everything. I discovered that Terri had gotten married to her friends' brother. I thought house sitting paid off for her. Her husband traveled a lot, and she suspected he was partying with women on his trips. She had that feeling, and T was always good at sensing things. They were on the edge of a divorce because her husband wanted to work in another state at a human resources division. He told Terri he could live there temporarily for about four months until the new office was up and running. Being Terri, she gave him an ultimatum to stay or leave. I didn't want to pry, and I could see she was very passionate and agitated, so I changed the subject.

Knowing Terri for all these years, I understood her. She would be loyal to her man, and she expected the same. She just wanted to be loved, and she would give back more than she received. That made us special because I had that same motivation. It could never be one-sided. It is hard to explain, but this lady knew what she wanted and wasn't much for settling for something less. We always had that air of excitement in everything we did. Even talking was never dull. We were quick to respond; she was a challenge, and whatever she gave in our relationship, I always wanted to do more. I told her she could do anything, and I saw her as an equal partner. The back and forth, the this for that, was truly magical. I couldn't get enough, and we did everything with passion. Our faces couldn't disguise our feelings, and we seemed to understand each other.

Her mind was always thinking two steps ahead. Sometimes, words came out of her mouth before her mind had processed them. But I could relate, and it was being too honest when we opened our mouths which some people hinking we were being judgemental. Terri could be intimidating to some people, but not to me. Through all her restlessness and thoughts, I always saw her as someone who wanted to be loved for herself. She had to be satisfied, and if you were going to be with her, you had to accept the whole package. She seemed complicated, but to me, she was simple to understand. That's why magic is an excellent way to describe our chemistry.

We spent the afternoon just as we had done before in East New York. Although many years had passed, our hearts didn't skip a beat. We laughed and had those embraces and touches that were electric. We stopped for a nightcap, and I didn't want the night to end. It was around 8 o'clock, and we had spent the better part of the day together. I drove her home. When we arrived, I wasn't sure how we would say goodnight. Terri invited me to take a tour of her home.

Of course, I obliged, and she was very proud of her home. I wasn't sure if her husband had lived there or if he had ownership. Terri didn't say much about this guy or any private details. I'm sure if I pressed, she would divulge, but it wasn't my place to ask, and it didn't matter. I regretted that I had an opportunity to be with her, but I didn't pull the trigger. I always had this feeling of being jealous that she was with other guys when she moved away. That was weird because what right did I have to feel that way? I felt that her failed marriage and the fact that our love never took that next step drove her away. I'm sure at one point, Terri loved her husband. She had a great home, a son, and a great job.

Everybody loves someone at some point in life. Then, you discover that your feelings and needs have changed, and you become restless. It was getting late, and I said I should be going. Terri said I could stay the night. I have already considered this situation and I have decided I would not take advantage of it. I would cheapen my true feelings for her. I found no value in a hit-and-run. That was too painful, and I felt I had damaged her heart enough. I should have and could have left my home many years ago, but I didn't.

Loyalty was something that had been instilled in me from my early days on the streets of the Bronx. My dad was a great example of how he toiled away at work for his family. I watched the wise guys and their code: a traitor is a rat, and nothing could be worse than being disloyal. As a teenager, I fought for myself, but in Vietnam, I learned that loyalty to the guys next to me was paramount.

If I were going to sleep with Terri, it would have to be forever, not just for a moment of pleasure. Georgia was recuperating from cancer, and one of the twins had moved into the city. My other son was in Georgetown, and if I left Georgia, what would that say about me? What would it say about me if I slept with Terri and went? I don't remember my exact words to Terri why I had to leave. It may have been a weak attempt to say that it would be too painful to be together and have to go the following day. I don't remember, but we embraced. It was one more passionate kiss and hug before we were at the door. My heart was breaking knowing I had signaled to her that we would never be together. I hurried to my car, and all the feeling of losses in relationships made my eyes well up. As I drove away, all those emotions and the thought of leaving a woman I loved drowned me in tears. I had to pull over about two or three blocks away, and I cried uncontrollably. I was bombarded with thoughts of how everything good goes away.

BACK TO BROOKLYN

The evening before had been very emotional, and I was drained emotionally. I made the trip back to Canarsie, Brooklyn. The twins had moved on, and Georgia was healing from cancer. The next few years without the kids gave us plenty of time to reconcile all the history that had never been fully resolved. We had friends that I had met in my early days when I dated Rosalie. Those friendships remained, and everyone's spouse got along with each other. We went to graduations and birthdays, and we took vacations together. Everyone's children were grown and living on their own. Life was moving along, and Georgia and I usually had weekend plans with a group of our friends. We would go to dinner or a show, sometimes a concert, and many times we hung out at someomes' home. Life wasn't bad, and I kept busy, but at certain times I thought of Terri.

I targeted 2008 as my retirement year. I would be 63 years old and planned to sell the house. I wanted to move away from New York to a tax-friendly state and a place with clean air. I was tired of the traffic, congestion, and filth of living in the city. The boys, Anthony and Michael, were doing well. Michael was working for a law firm in Maryland. Anthony had gotten married and was living in lower Manhattan by the Brooklyn Bridge. It had been several years since I saw Terri in Bethesda. I was sure she found someone, and she never contacted me, nor did I try to contact her.

I was at work in midtown Manhattan, and a secretary announced that a plane had hit the World Trade Center. Anthony's office was in a smaller building at the Trade Center. At first, the details were sketchy. But within a few minutes, it was clear that this was not a small plane that lost its way. I was about to call Georgia at the house, but she was already on the phone trying to reach Anthony. I finally got through and told her to calm down. She panicked because he didn't answer her call at work. I told her there could be a lot of reasons why he didn't answer. I told her to call his apartment; maybe he was still home. We found out that he was at a meeting further down on Wall Street, but we didn't find that out for a few hours.

When the second plane hit the towers, all hell broke loose. My office had a lounge area with a TV, and several executives had TVs in their offices. I saw the second plane hit the tower, and we all stood there with our mouths open in disbelief. I thought we were at war when a second plane struck the World Trade Center. Flashbacks of being on the Huey under fire darted in my mind. I had not thought about that day when I got hit, and our Huey was almost annihilated. I can't even discuss all the fallout that affected me and Georgia with the collapse of the Twin Towers. Georgia had friends from high school in New Jersey. Two of her friends died on the upper floors of the towers. Both friends had children who were still living at home. I lost friends, but my hardened heart from Vietnam kept my feelings suppressed.

Life is a roller coaster, and like the cyclone at Coney Island, life has twists and turns and ups and downs. You always hope the coaster never falls off track. But that is what happened a few weeks after September 11th. It was a Saturday, and I had gone to the car wash. Georgia and I planned on picking up some friends for the movies, and I wanted a clean car. Everyone was still reeling from 9/11 and needed a night out with our friends.

I returned from the car wash, and I found Georgia face down on the living room floor when I arrived home. I didn't panic, and from my Vietnam experience, everything seemed to be in slow motion. I rolled her onto her back. I cleared her airway, but her breathing was extremely shallow. I performed chest compressions. Clearing her airway and performing CPR improved her breathing. But she didn't communicate, and her eyes were open but were not moving. She had a nasty weld and was bleeding on the side of her head. I knew I needed an ambulance and help, and I called 911. It seemed like it took forever, but it was only minutes when a team of paramedics arrived and took over.

The ambulance took Georgia to Brookdale Hospital. I followed the ambulance in my car. She had a stroke and had also hit her head in the fall. The doctors told me that the next 24 hours would be critical. They performed all types of tests to determine if her brain was functioning. I called Anthony, and he and his wife arrived at the hospital quickly. They came from their Manhattan apartment. I called Michael in Maryland and told him to stay put until tomorrow. He told me he would get on a flight tonight. If not, Mike would be home on Sunday. I stayed at the hospital overnight and sent Anthony and his wife back to their place.

The next afternoon, the doctor told me she could hear us. Her speech was slowed and almost nonexistent, but they said it would improve. Likewise, she may experience memory loss, affecting her long- and short-term memories. That didn't sound great, but she was not in danger of dying. I feared how long it would take for her to recover and if her rehabilitation could bring her back to normal. Georgia became more robust each day, and her motor skills improved. The speech was slow, and it was so sad to watch someone have her life altered in the blink of an eye. Her life changed, and she was functioning at less than fifty percent.

Georgia was hospitalized for weeks and moved to a rehab center for several more weeks. My boss at AT&T was great, and I was at the hospital and rehab center every day. Georgia had made good progress, and her speech was back to a regular cadence, but she did have some memory issues. I reflected on how our lives had changed again. All the plans and thoughts of retiring and moving to enjoy our retirement years didn't matter. During the next two years, Georgia seemed to recover, but she didn't remember many things and sometimes forgot that Michael had moved to Maryland. She would try to hide the fact that her memory had slipped.

I was more concerned that she might forget to turn off the gas on the stove while I was at work. I was also worried that she might forget where she parked the car when shopping. I still took her to the doctor every two months as a follow-up. Sadly, after seemingly making a remarkable comeback, signs of Alzheimer's appeared. I'll never forget our family's problematic decision that we didn't want to face, but the handwriting was on the wall. It was evident that she needed care just to do simple tasks. We decided to place Georgia in an assisted living home. It was precisely three years after her fall that I took her to a facility in Staten Island, NY.

Georgia's mind had forgotten a lot, and she couldn't be left alone to go to stores, cook, and do everyday chores. There was always the fear that she would hurt herself. I would visit her on Saturday or Sunday, depending on when Anthony and his wife would see her. Michael took a vacation or a long weekend to stay at my house, and we would visit Georgia. She looked great, and no one would ever think she was having trouble. Georgia ambulated freely. That was impressive, considering her age, the stroke, and the circumstances of her fall. She could have a good conversation. Still, there always came a point where she would get lost in her situation. One time, when Michael and I visited, she thought Mike was a doctor. That was hard to swallow. After about a year, she was slipping away, and she ate less and needed help changing her clothes and washing. I would bring her flowers, stuffed animals, rice pudding, and a candy bar she always loved.

The sad part is that she sometimes thought I was the delivery man. I wasn't sorry for myself; I felt terrible that someone so kind and giving was trapped in a make-believe world. But she was happy and was not in pain. Toward the end, she wouldn't eat and didn't want to get out of bed. It seemed she had lost the will to continue. It was sad to watch a person deteriorate in front of your eyes. Such a sweet and giving person and mother of twins was now a shell of her former self. I knew the end was near, and I just prayed that she would be at peace and slip away without pain.

It was at the end of 2005 that she slipped into a coma. Her brain had no activity, so I decided to call the boys. I told them to come home, and we would choose to let her go to sleep. Her boys were with her as the doctors removed her from life support.

BYE BYE

My retirement date was approaching, and I was intent on leaving Brooklyn. My dad passed away in 2000, and my two sisters and their families moved to the Atlantic City area. They moved to Absecon, NJ; one sister bought a mother-daughter home and watched over mom. I started to look at Wildwood, NJ, and Cape May, NJ. New developments were being built in Smithville, NJ, only a few miles from Absecon. I took a lot of weekend trips to search the area and got some gambling done in AC. I found a great community, and there were three models left. I bought a two-bedroom, two-bathroom house on one level with a two-car garage.

I decided to leave AT&T in 2008. I had worked for both New York Telephone and AT&T for 20 years. I sold the house in Canarsie and received five times what I had paid for it when I bought it. I bought a new home in a great community. My taxes were minimal, and I was in great financial shape. Mom died in the summer of 2009, and I felt like my life had turned a new chapter. I didn't seem to have a care in the world. I was healthy and wanted to share my good fortune with a woman. I thought back to my earliest days after high school when I wanted to meet a girl from the suburbs. She would be from a more privileged upbringing than me and the kids from the streets in the Bronx. I never found that, but I had become successful beyond my wildest imagination. I wanted a good time and swore I would not marry again. I wanted to have those girlfriends who were close but had their own space.

I lived in an adult community that offered many activities. I met a divorcee a few years younger than me who had bought in the first phase of building in the development. We had a brief romance, but we each wanted to be free, which was fine with me. But within months of hanging out with each other, she decided she was moving to Sarasota, Florida. See, nothing good ever sticks around.

Another few years passed, and I always remembered the many great times I had growing up in the Bronx and living in Brooklyn. My relationship with Terri always brought cheer to my mind. Our magical love affair never left my mind, But at times, I felt lonely. I had three good pals from Brooklyn: Frankie, Phil, and Ronnie; we would get together monthly. We would howl in laughter at all the crazy times we had living in Brooklyn. I learned how to play golf. Can you imagine a kid from the Bronx going to play golf? I joined a bowling league and an over-sixty softball team. I think I did all these things to forget a lot of heartache. If you have been paying attention to Mikey's story, you know about many of my loves and losses which have impacted who I am today. I am still here, and God must have a purpose and plan for me.

A few more years passed, and I had some medical issues, some related to my wounds and service in Vietnam. Time is flying by, and it is ten years after 9/11, and Georgia died six years ago.

I started to make a bucket list. The number one item on the list is to get back on board a Huey. I don't know how that would feel, but something called me to sit in the well again. I visited the Smithsonian Museum, and the section about America's wars had a Huey on display. I froze, and I was in a trance. I forgot how flimsy the cabin was constructed and how vulnerable the crew was to enemy fire. I have to get on a Huey one more time.

The second item has many parts because I want to see Rosalie again. I'd like to see how things turned out for her. Christina and Roxy pop into my mind, and I want to know what happened to them.

Lastly, and just as important as my Huey ride, I would like to know what Terri is doing. Is she happy? Is she with someone? Are any of these people alive today? Just to see her one more time would complete the list. But what if seeing her wasn't enough? I began using my cell phone more socially and even joined Facebook. I had reservations about exposing information, but I found it to be a great source for locating these people. Either I didn't know how to negotiate the platform, or they weren't participating because I couldn't find anyone, which only made me think of them more.

I reconnected with Marco from the phone company and talked about our lives and whatever happened to this guy or that gal. Of course, I asked about Terri, but he had no information to offer. I accidentally found Marco on a Facebook page for former NY Telephone employees. I met Marco and some guys I had worked with in East New York for lunch in Staten Island.

Time moved forward, and I turned sixty-six. I never imagined I would still be living and growing up. I thought by the time I was sixty, I'd be sitting on a park bench, feeding the squirrels. But I had energy, made new friends, and reconnected with old acquaintances. One evening, I was scrolling on Facebook and saw something about an AT&T page for retirees. I had become friends on Facebook with some people that I had worked with at AT&T in Manhattan. Someone had started a conversation about the oldies and music from the 60's and 70's. Terry Brown commented on having the time of her life, and I answered back that it was the best time.

The next day, I got a facebook message that said, Mikey? Did you have the time of your life? I immediately knew this was T, even though her name was spelled Terry and her last name was Brown. My heart skipped a beat. I didn't want to write too much, even though the message was private. I told her to call if she wanted and gave her my cell phone number. Terri said she would try to reach me the next day.

AFTER ALL THESE YEARS

The next day, I was loading my car with groceries, and my phone rang. I was shocked because Terri's unmistakable voice was on the line. I could hardly believe that after all these years, I was talking to Terri. To be blunt and honest, I never thought we would speak again. As usual, we talked for a long time; there was much to catch up on and discuss.

I told Terri that Georgia had died before I retired and that I concentrated on finishing my career and moving away from Brooklyn and NYC. I wanted to start a new chapter in my life. Everything that has happened since childhood in the Bronx to the present time is filled with precious memories. There was also an immense amount of sadness, and I confessed to Terri that she never left my mind. I reminded her that I always told her she could do anything, and obviously, she had a great career and her share of love lost relationships. After all the time between us, I was sure that whatever she did was on her terms. I was alone, and I wanted to know how she was doing and if she was happy. In the back of my mind, I hoped she was free, but I saw her last name was Brown. I assumed that she married again and that this time was the charm.

Terri told me she was on her third marriage and had met a man who worked for Time Warner. They had met during projects between AT&T and Time Warner. He had lived in Potomac, Maryland, and they would spend time together. That went on for a while, and when she retired, Terri bought a home outside of Clemson, SC. She said she wanted to be close to the mountains and lakes. Terri had a house built at the foot of the Smokey Mountains, and the area had many recreational lakes. It was a new community, and she felt that if she sold her home in Bethesda and moved in with her steady boyfriend, she had a fallback plan. If things didn't work out, she could rely on moving to South Carolina. Terri always took care of Terri. Terri retired in 2009 and had her dream home completed the same year. She would spend some time there and also with her partner in Potomac. They got married that same year. Her home was already built in South Carolina, and her husband sold his home in Maryland..

She seemed happy and willing to take a third attempt at marriage. We rehashed our past and our present situations. We concluded that, for all the chemistry we shared, our timing in life had us in different places. It's

20-plus years later, and our positions are reversed. I was alone, and she was married. She said she wanted to talk again and stay in touch. I told her I was unencumbered and that she could call me anytime. It was hard to hang up, and it seemed neither of us wanted to hang up first. We kept saying bye to each other, but the line stayed open. I finally said, OK, I will hang up first, but it's not goodbye; I'll see you. So, the call ended, and I had to sit another ten minutes in the parking lot to assess the last seventy-five minutes.

I had Terri's cell phone number to text or private message her on Facebook. I would never call without first making sure she was alone. So many years had passed, but the thought of us being together never left, and time seemed to heal those wounds. But after this call, I wanted more, and after hearing her Brooklyn's voice made me feel like we were bantering just like it was yesterday. Yet she was married and had been with her new husband for many years, so I thought she had found the love she needed. Knowing T, I felt she wouldn't settle, and her husband must have checked off all the boxes that satisfied her desires.

I decided to text her for a week, but I wanted to hear her voice. She texted back and said the next day would be better to talk when she went shopping. I said okay, and she called me. We talked about the kids and how they had grown up and been successful. Her son had a boy and a girl, so she was a grandmother. That sounded strange since I never thought of her as grandma. I told her that Michael wasn't married, and Anthony and his wife, Maria, hadn't started a family.

Terri was thrilled with her new home and living in the western section of South Carolina. Getting away from the rat race and congestion of the DC area was a breath of fresh air. The climate was very moderate. There was no snow and mild winters, but the summer months were hot and could have stretches of humidity. But she planned to travel during the summer. Terri always had a plan, and although she could be a homebody, she had that restless energy to explore.

I told her I lived close to Atlantic City and the Jersey and Delaware shores. The adult community where I lived had many activities, and most residents were transplants from NYC and Northern NJ. The only drawback was the cold weather from January through March. I never traveled much, but Terri perked my curiosity about living in a more moderate climate. I had friends and acquaintances who retired and moved to Florida, or they bought a property and spent the winters in Florida. The more I thought about Terri living in South Carolina, the more I thought about escaping the damp and cold winter in the Northeast.

I was in good financial shape, so I started to look at Florida as an option. I had never been to Florida, so I talked to friends who moved there or had a second home. I knew little about which coast was the best fit for me. After much discussion and pondering, I purchased a home in an adult association. I wouldn't have to take care of the grounds, and I had a small screened-in backyard. The house was detached and had a two-car garage. It was perfect; it had two full baths, and everything was on one floor. It was outside of Tampa and part of Lakeland, Florida. It wasn't far from the Orlando Airport and far away from storm surges during hurricane season. I also looked at the map and saw it was about nine hours from Terri in South Carolina.

My mind hoped beyond a reasonable chance that I would see her again, and I began to talk more often with her. She and her husband were retired, but their communication had slipped. I understood that because that's how I felt about Georgia after we started to raise a family. But I didn't think she would leave her husband after all the time they had been together. I would like to get another chance with Terri. Boy, the shoe was on the other foot.

Terri and I talked more often, and she confided to me that hearing my voice stirred her memory. She felt like she wanted another chance for us to be together. We could always speak our minds, and sometimes what we said was brutally honest. But we understood each other, and we would never throw away our feelings over a discussion or disagreement.

Our talks lasted longer and more frequent. We remembered songs, that movie, and what a great time we had living, working, and growing up in Brooklyn. Without making any verbal pact, we began to text each other to say goodnight every night. I just couldn't get enough. And those words reminded me of a Barry White song. We liked the same music, and sometimes our connection was so strong that hearing a lyric put us immediately in the same place. We were hot-wired, and the current was as strong as ever after all these years.

JUST TO SEE HER

We communicated for several years. I am nearly 70, and Terri is in her sixties. We still have that fire and spirit; we would be dynamic if we were together. As time passed, I wanted to see her at least once more. It was on my bucket list. I told her and didn't know if she would accept that notion. She said that she changed and gained some weight. I told her that most women gain weight and that I didn't care.

I thought of various schemes to get us together. I would be passing through the western part of South Carolina. I was headed to the west coast of Florida for the winter. Nothing would get us together, and another year clicked forward. I heard a Smokey Robinson song on the radio. It was titled Just to See Her, and boy, that fit. The lyrics are: "To see her face and her warm embrace, just to see her again." "I would do anything, go anywhere, just to be with her again." Those words may not be the exact lyrics. But they capture the feeling and intention of my heart. I long to hear the melody of these beautiful lyrics. I wanted that long embrace and to see her smiling face.

We always had eye contact and big grins when we looked at each other. My face felt as though it would crack from smiling so hard. I needed to refresh my sense of her fragrance. The touch of her hands or mine holding her face always made me forget where I was for thirty seconds. Honestly, it was like I melted into her arms. I would say these things in my messages, and her response left no doubt that she felt the same way. I would say I love you to the moon and back, and she would say I love you more. Our banter would dual each other, trying to say we would do more for each other. That's how we were, which is still how we feel. I couldn't believe it. It is MAGIC! How else can I describe it?

Just before my seventy-first birthday, I was headed back from my winter vacation in Lakeland, Florida. I decided to let her know I would be passing close by on my way back to Smithville, New Jersey. I could alter the route or the day I was leaving Florida. I was flexible if it would mean the possibility of us seeing each other. She called me and said she had appointments at a particular time and place. She asked if I would be passing by around that time. My response was that I would make it my business to rendezvous. We searched the area to find a place to get something to eat and agreed to meet for brunch. I was thrilled, but there was some apprehension. What if all this texting didn't translate when we looked at each other? What if I didn't feel her emotions like I did so many years ago? I didn't let that cloud my mind, and I had to know these answers. Maybe, at some point, we would be back together. Stranger things have happened to me in life.

I found my way to our planned location, and by chance, I pulled up a car away from her, but I didn't notice her. We called each other as we were approaching our planned stop. I said," Hey T, I'm here, and she said I know I see you; you're right in front of me. I said, "Where?" She said to look behind. It felt like this was how we always talked. We exited the cars, and that big grin was on my mug. I wrestled with the idea of whether I should kiss her and how I should kiss her. I wasn't sure that it would be proper since she was married. A peck on the cheek wouldn't do her right. So I just put my arms around her and gave her a solid yet soft hug. It lasted a long time as we laughed. I buried my head next to hers and held the hug. I would lift my head and back off to see her smiling face. We grinned, we laughed some more, and I went back for that warm embrace. I wanted to spin her around but thought us old folks might get hurt. We kept hugging in the parking lot like we were teenagers.

We went into the restaurant and ordered breakfast. We sat across from each other. We couldn't believe that after all these years, we're sitting together for breakfast, just like we did many years ago." At one point, I walked around the table to sit beside Terri and had the waitress take a picture of my cell phone. I felt the same vibe as I did when we first met. We probably overstayed our welcome at the table, and she had to finish her chores, so we returned to our cars. It took a while to finally say goodbye and separate from the several long hugs. I think I said something like the next time we meet, but I can't remember because the emotions of holding her overpowered me.

We got in our cars and pulled out of the lot. At the corner, we stopped for the light, and when the light turned green, she went right, and I went left. I think I smiled for the next ten miles. I made an overnight stop, and we texted each other at the end of the evening, as we had done for the last few years.

Just to see her and hold her in my arms that one time would never be enough. I was so happy that my dream of seeing and holding her again had come true. I should be satisfied because that's all I asked for, but it would be grand to keep her forever.

I thought I was fortunate because this was one of two things I had to do on my bucket list. How many people are so lucky to reunite with someone they love after twenty years? Even though it may have been for 90 minutes, I will hold that feeling for Terri with all my other emotions in my heart forever.

I don't know what will happen in the future. As you have read, my life has traveled down many avenues, and life constantly changes. I cannot be disappointed, and I probably could have died many times in Vietnam. All the changes I have experienced in life are bonuses. All the trials that I have experienced in life have made me stronger.

I was never a religious person, but I always felt that God would take me through any situation. I felt that Jesus was my co-pilot in Vietnam. All the losses of friends and my own injuries that happened in Nam seemed almost insurmountable. The lost relations with Ro and Christina at the time seemed like I would never walk with that girl of my dreams.

I believe that through it all God had a plan and I had been blessed with a marriage that produced two boys who are doing well, and even though Georgia passed onto the grave, we both needed each other at a certain point in our lives.

I returned to my home in Smithville and celebrated my seventy-first birthday. I know one thing: I don't know what life will bring in the next year. I know that Terri and I text each other and support each other. It never leaves my mind that maybe I will see Terri again. Terri will always and forever be in my life. The unknown answer is, will we ever live together? I will never stop believing that we might. Strange things have happened in my life.

THE END

EPILOGUE

Francis Michael DeNatale lives today in a fictional realm. But Mikey represents many people who have experienced similar events in their lives. He was part of the baby-boomer generation. His experiences transcend many generations. Everyone can identify with some aspect of his heartache and triumphs. As his author, I decided to let you think and decide what would happen to him. I didn't want the story to end happily ever after. In the real world, not everyone finds what they are looking for. It could take a lifetime of struggles and heartache to be at peace. What will Mikey do? Do Terri and Mikey live a magical life together at some point? Will Mikey continue to grow and find someone else, or maybe no one? That's life questions, folks, and no one knows. What is going to be your story? Where are you going, and where have you been on the coaster of life? What do you seek?

Maybe you have watched people go through some or all the situations that Mikey experienced. Perhaps you had similar experiences and can relate to how life changes your course. Maybe Mikey finally stopped to smell the coffee. After all his years of trying to live with worldly solutions and pleasures, he found that faith in God was what he really needed.

I know that everything in this world will end, and you will return to dust—the dead know nothing. The dead don't see or hear; they quietly sleep. Maybe Mikey can find peace. You decide his fate and your own!

ACKNOWLEDGEMENT

Nadine Mass put me on a path that led me to write this story. A veteran and army officer, Nadine was the director of the Veteran Center in East Harlem. She was also my clinician and established a writing group for veterans. Her support never wavered, and other veterans and I found a safe place to share our feelings and experiences. Our group talked about Vietnam and the military. We did it through the power of the pen. Nadine suggested that I join the group, and as it's said, the rest is history. Since 2018, writing warriors have continued to express themselves through writing. I published my first book in 2020, a memoir, and that encouragement from the group and Nadine led me to produce this fictional adventure story. Thank you, Nadine. I was so fortunate to have you as my counselor. Thank you for your service and all you do for veterans.

Kate Ellis was an integral member of our team when Ms. Mass started the group. Kate is a retired professor of English at Rutgers University. She is also an author in her own right. She provided technical support, and she dedicated her time to this cause. Kate encouraged me to write and dig deep into my experiences. She always offered suggestions and edits to polish my work. Every week, Kate would review my work and provide recommendations and corrections. Thank you, Kate, for giving your time freely to support our group and pushing me to give more.

To Meade, Gary, and Tom, my brothers in service and members of this group, thank you for your encouragement. Thanks for your feedback and taking an interest in this project. Thank you for sharing your story, which inspired me to create this book.

Sarah Bohannon, LCSW, DSW, and veteran, thank you for moderating our group each week. Thank you for your encouragement. I genuinely appreciate your motivation, and I thank you for your service in the US Navy. Thank you for your honest feedback. You keep our group on track and have helped support this endeavor. Your care for our well-being is noticeable and speaks to your dedication.

ABOUT THE AUTHOR

This book is Frank's second published work. His first was a memoir titled You Can Never Go Home, which was completed in 2020. Frank was born in May 1948, in the Bay Ridge section of Brooklyn, New York, and attended St. Johns Prep High School. He wrote a few articles for his school newspaper, mainly covering sports at St. John's. Although he had an interest in journalism, Frank never attended college. Instead, he joined the army and found himself in Vietnam. Frank served in the III Corps from April 1968 to April 1969. He served in a service company, part of the 610th Maintenance Battalion.

Frank had two stints playing baseball in Florida. He made his first attempt at baseball in the summer of 1967, before going to Vietnam. He made another attempt in 1972 after returning home. He left the army in August 1970 after reaching the rank of Specialist Five. He held various jobs, from an office setting to factory . In May 1973, he was called by the US Postal Service in Brooklyn, and his career lasted until labor2010. Working from the ground up, he was promoted to Director of Operations for the Brooklyn PO in 1988. He was the acting manager at the mail processing facility in Hackensack, NJ. He was also the officer-in-charge of the Great Neck and Staten Island Post Offices in New York. In 1992, Frank became the Postmaster in Jersey City. In the last six years of his service, he adjudicated labor cases for the Northern New Jersey District.

In 1988, Frank volunteered to coach ice hockey. He coached at every youth level, including a women's 19 and under team. He coached at Wagner College, and he spent almost twenty years at Montclair State University. He worked as an assistant coach, head coach, and associate head coach before retiring in 2023.

Frank lives in New Jersey with his wife. His two children each have two grandchildren. Frank enjoys the winters in Florida. He serves on the condo association board. He participates weekly with his writing group.

Milton Keynes UK
Ingram Content Group UK Ltd.
UKHW050741040324
438876UK00007B/166